MAGGIE CASPER

O'Malley Wild

Tangled Sheets

ELLORA'S CAVE
ROMANTICA PUBLISHING

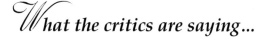 *What the critics are saying...*

ΕΟ

Hayden's Hellion

4 Hearts "Maggie Casper has a way of creating sexy dominant men that capture the reader and hold them captive. [...] Love scenes are hotter than hot and the first book in the series is a must read. I can't wait to see what Maggie Casper comes up with for the next book in the series." ~ *The Romance Studio*

Tying the Knot

"Maggie Casper's trademark eroticism comes in to play in Tying the Knot.[...] If you've read the O'Malley trilogy, you know how hunky and loving the three grooms are, and as they get ready to be husbands, you'll see once again how much love and admiration they hold for their brides. Tying the Knot proves to be a fitting conclusion for such a sexy and exciting trilogy." ~ *The Romance Studio*

An Ellora's Cave Romantica Publication

www.ellorascave.com

Tangled Sheets

ISBN 9781419955440
ALL RIGHTS RESERVED.
Hayden's Hellion Copyright © 2005 Maggie Casper
Tying the Knot Copyright © 2005 Maggie Casper
Edited by Mary Moran.
Cover art by Syneca.

This book printed in the U.S.A. by Jasmine–Jade Enterprises, LLC.

Trade paperback Publication September 2007

Excerpt from *Sex, Spies and Sapphire* Copyright © Shelley Munro, 2007

Also by Maggie Casper

ഇ

About the Author

80

Maggie Casper's life could be called many things but boring isn't one of them. If asked, Maggie would tell you that blessed would more aptly describe her everyday existence.

Being loved by four gorgeous daughters should be enough to make anybody feel blessed. Add to that a bit of challenge, a lot of fun and an undeniably close circle of friends and family and you'd be walking in her shoes.

A love of reading was passed on by Maggie's mother at a very early age, and so began her addiction to romance novels. Maggie admits to writing some in high school but when life got in the way, she put her pen and paper up. Seems that things changed over the years because when she finally decided it was time to put her story ideas on paper, the pen was out and the computer was in. Took her a while to catch up but she finally made it.

When not writing, Maggie can usually be found reading, doing genealogy research or watching NASCAR.

Maggie welcomes comments from readers. You can find her website and email address on her author bio page at www.ellorascave.com.

Tell Us What You Think

We appreciate hearing reader opinions about our books. You can email us at Comments@EllorasCave.com.

TANGLED SHEETS

ℰꙅ

HAYDEN'S HELLION
~13~

&

TYING THE KNOT
~127~

HAYDEN'S HELLION

ജ

Dedication

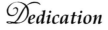

To my editor Mary Moran, thank you for your patience and kindness, but most of all, thank you for believing in me.

Trademarks Acknowledgement

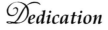

The author acknowledges the trademarked status and trademark owners of the following wordmarks mentioned in this work of fiction:

Chevy Caprice Classic: General Motors Corporation

Stetson: John B. Stetson Company

NASCAR: National Association for Stock Car Auto Racing, Inc.

Chapter One

ဢ

She descended the courthouse steps mumbling to herself. *Get a real job,* she mimicked in the snottiest tone she could muster, trying for the same no-nonsense tone Judge Gumar had used on her not more than thirty minutes ago. She'd known the old goat since she was knee-high to a June bug and she still wanted to wring his damned neck.

At twenty-four, Austin Calhoun was about as wild as the Old West. She enjoyed having fun and could care less what others thought of her. She had an independent streak a mile wide and figured it wasn't her problem if the old biddies in town didn't like the fact she made her money holding sensual parties. Hell, they probably wouldn't know what a vibrator was if they sat on one.

Just because she didn't dress in fancy clothes and run off to an office every morning didn't mean her job wasn't legitimate. She received a very nice quarterly check. It might not be enough for a lot of extra things, but she was a simple woman happy living a simple life.

As long as she had the necessities, she would be fine. A bit of extra gas money for Jolene and she was doing wonderful. After all, Jolene had been with her through the good and the bad. Just as good as any friend and usually a lot more fun, her maroon nineteen-seventy-six Chevy Caprice Classic was fast and sleek and could glide over the roughest terrain without fussing a bit.

Of course, it was also the same vehicle that kept her in trouble with Judge Gumar. Just because she had a penchant for speeding and an accumulation of tickets due to that fact, didn't make her a menace to society as the judge claimed.

"Son of a bitchin' asshole," she mumbled, continuing her tirade as she stomped to her car. "I ought to drive Jolene right up his fat ass..."

Her bitch-a-thon was cut short when she ran into a brick wall—only this brick wall had arms. Both of those arms were wrapped around her like steel bands, tight and unbending. Whoever it was may have just been trying to steady her, but instead, she felt penned in, which added to her flaming temper, pissing her off even more.

Her struggles ceased when the breath was squeezed from her lungs. The stranger holding her set her back at arm's length.

"Settle down," was the growled command.

Stiffening as she recognized the voice, Austin slowly tilted her head back to see if she was right. Did the gravely voice belong to Hayden O'Malley? Tipping it even further, she followed the expanse of his broad chest until she was staring into hazel eyes so cold they could chill even the hottest Texas day.

"I should have known," she bit out as she separated herself from his grasp. "Started out a bad day, might as well fuck it up real proper-like," she said as she propped her hands on the generous swell of her hips.

From the top of his hat to the toe of his scuffed boots, Hayden O'Malley was cowboy through and through, the last of a dying breed. His jeans fit him like a second skin. Faded white in just the right spots, they were sexy as hell.

The way his blue snap-front chambray shirt was stretched taut across his chest made her mouth water. Damn, what she wouldn't give to ride him like the wind. Carefree and wild, it would be a momentous occasion.

"I don't know what's eating you, little girl, but don't you go taking it out on me. And I warned you about that nasty mouth of yours." His voice was low, ominous. It grated across her flesh as she imagined his five o'clock stubble would, invigorating every nerve ending in the process.

"Don't go gettin' all high and mighty on me, Hayden. I'm a grown-ass woman now and I'll thank you to remember that. Besides, I've got every reason to be mad."

"Not a good enough reason for the filth spilling from your mouth. You still aren't too big to paddle even if you are a woman now," he said, looking down at her from his towering height.

Sometimes being short sucked. Her five-foot, two-inch frame looked dwarfed next to Hayden's six-foot height. It was one of the many things that attracted her to the rugged rancher.

"Oh, hell, Hayden, when are you gonna get over it. I was nine years old the last time you whipped my ass. I don't sneak cigarettes anymore so you accomplished your task."

"I'd say from the sound of it you're due another round." He sounded as if his patience was running short. It was probably a good time to back off just a bit. The man always followed through with a threat, and she had no desire to have her ass paddled in front of half the town.

"All right already, calm down," she said giving him a mischievous grin. "I'll behave."

His eyes searched her face, their hazel depths cool and calculating as they studied her. The corners were lined, adding to his rugged masculinity.

"I somehow doubt that, darlin'," he drawled. "You come stomping from the courthouse in a huff mumbling under your breath. I'd say you haven't been behavin' at all."

His large hand reached out and grasped her elbow forcing her to move with him. His touch was gentle yet firm. His warm palm against her skin made it tingle. The sensation ran up her arm before tumbling the length of her body, ultimately settling deep inside her core.

"You know how he is, Hayden."

She was cut short by his snort of laughter. "What was it this time? Speeding?" he asked.

A bit embarrassed, she could feel her cheeks heat. "I had a party in the next county that lasted longer than I planned. I was late getting home and tired so I rushed." It sounded like a perfectly excusable excuse to her, but the deputy and the judge didn't agree.

"Let me get this straight. You were out alone on a deserted highway late at night driving while half-asleep when you got pulled over?" He was starting to sound angry and that wasn't at all good. She opened her mouth to speak, but he stared her down. Glaring at him, she snapped her jaw closed.

"You're lucky you don't belong to me. You wouldn't be able to sit for a week."

The arrogant beast! "First of all, women aren't belongings and second of all, I'm not a child who can be spanked for acting up so just chill the hell out."

She watched in utter fascination as his eyebrows snapped together. The step he took toward her was controlled but she could tell he was on the verge of being irate. Taking a step back, she couldn't help but wonder what it would be like to be punished by Hayden O'Malley.

Her traitorous body hummed with the idea. Her pussy became wet making her panties damp. The throbbing ache of her clit had her thinking of the little buzzing toy she kept in the glove box of Jolene. If she couldn't have the real thing she'd settle for something battery-operated.

"Watch how you look at a man, Hellion. You're all but asking me to take you to my bed with those blue eyes of yours. One of these days you might turn those baby blues on the wrong man and get more than you bargained for."

Shaking her head, she tried to clear all the wicked thoughts from her mind. She absently wondered if Hayden could give her more than she bargained for?

"So what did you get this time, community service? It's got to be something real good to have you throwing such a fit."

He was enjoying himself way too much, there had to be something she could do to put him in his place. He was a hard man who didn't trust easily. He had no use for women except to warm his bed, and he had no qualms about speaking his mind on the subject.

He was larger than life and devastatingly handsome, but that was where the good ended. Once you made it past his looks, he was worse than most—stubborn as a mule and much too conservative.

He liked his women meek and biddable and had old-fashioned beliefs. It was probably a good thing he'd never encouraged her. With her wild independent streak, she'd forever have a sore ass.

Her blue eyes captivated him. They shone with innocence even though he knew better. Hell, half the town knew better, the other half knew firsthand, but that didn't stop him from wondering what it would be like to hold her curvy body against his throughout the night.

It bothered him that she could wrap herself so tightly around him leaving him hard and ready every time. He was a man in control and would remain that way. Once, long ago, he'd given his heart and soul to a woman. Not much more than a boy himself at the time, the pain had been unbearable. He'd vowed then never to love, never to trust, and so far it had been easy, but there was something about the way Austin looked at him. The way she reacted to his closeness warned him to stay as far away from her as possible.

"Well?" he insisted.

She gave him an irritated look. "What are you doing in town?" she asked, obviously trying to change the subject.

"Came in for some supplies but that doesn't matter. What matters is you answer my question."

"Fine then," she huffed. "The damned jackass told me I had to have a real job by the end of the week or I'll be spending thirty days in his jail." Her foot was tapping—her tiny hands with their plump fingers had once again balled into fists and were resting on her hips. Hips he could hold tight to as he thrust deeply into the tight clasp of her soaking wet pussy.

Damn! He swore silently. *Where in the hell had that come from?*

"Can you believe that shit? Now what in the hell am I going to do?"

He wasn't sure whether to coddle her or wash her mouth out with soap. "First of all you can watch your language. I won't warn you again." He hoped his voice sounded stern.

Before his brain had time to engage, his mouth had spit out the words. "You can come work for me keeping my books."

She looked almost as surprised as he felt. Then her mouth broke into a wide smile showing a full set of white teeth. Her lush lips were coated with peach gloss. He wondered if it would make her mouth taste like peaches. And would it come off if she were to drop to her knees in front of him and stretch her full lips around the head of his cock?

Good Lord! Get a grip, he chided himself.

She squealed as she launched herself at him. "Thank you, Hayden. I promise I'll do good, you just watch and see if I don't."

Narrowing his eyes, he set her away from him and prayed she hadn't felt his engorged length as it vied for freedom from the confines of his jeans.

"How long do you need a job?" *Please let it be short-term,* he begged.

"The judge said I had to have a steady job for at least six months and if I got another ticket in that time, I'd be in big trouble. You know what, Hayden? I think he means it this time."

"I'll give you a job, but it'll be on my terms. What I say goes, so it would be in your best interest to watch that sassy mouth of yours and tread lightly."

He could tell she had a hard-core retort all lined up but must have thought better of it. Although her eyes shot blue daggers, she said nothing.

There would be many things he would address while she worked for him. For one, she wouldn't be traipsing around the ranch half-dressed. He looked her over from head to toe, which wasn't a long way.

In height, Austin Calhoun was a tiny woman. What she lacked in height she made up for over and over again in womanly attributes. Her cherubic face was lightly freckled, making her upturned nose seem pixie-like. Both cheeks dimpled deeply when she smiled, and she smiled a lot. Bright red hair stuck up every which way, there was no telling what color it would be next week, and for the life of him, he couldn't remember what color it had been last week.

She preferred clothes better suited for a hooker, and thought nothing of the fact. She'd just come from a court of law wearing a black T-shirt with a picture of a cowboy half-dressed. Below the picture was the inscription *"Save a horse, ride a cowboy"*.

Bet the judge loved that one, he thought wryly.

It was stretched tightly across the largest set of breasts he'd ever seen. Of course, he'd only ever seen them clothed. They were definitely real, it just seemed she'd never grown into them. Her waist narrowed briefly before her hips curved out. She was voluptuous but didn't seem to care that she didn't fit in with the latest style. Her confidence made her a very attractive package.

The skirt was short enough to hint at what was below. Made a man want to drop something at her feet to see whether she'd stoop or bend. Either way, someone would get a free show.

Her skin was smooth and tan. He knew she was often spotted sunbathing in front of her trailer or at the lake. He'd not had the pleasure of seeing her in a swimsuit in years, but often heard what a view it was.

She grabbed his arm bringing him out of his lust-induced daydream. "Come on, Hayden. Let's go tell Judge Gumar the good news."

Her excitement evident, she bounced beside him, causing her breasts to sway and jiggle beneath the shirt.

"Just remember what I said, darlin', my way, on my terms. I won't put up with any of your crap. You cause me any grief, and I'll see to it you're too sore to sit for a mighty long time."

She said nothing in return although he could almost see the smoke billowing from her ears. It was going to be an interesting six months. The one thing that bothered him was the fact she could have his blood pounding south of his belt buckle without even trying.

He needed to remember that she wasn't his type. When he finally decided to settle down, it would be for companionship and children—love or true emotion would have no part in it. It would also do him good to remember the rumors that had followed Austin Calhoun over the years. The one thing he didn't want was to fall for a woman who had slept with every young buck in town.

With those thoughts firmly imbedded in his mind, if not in his groin, he followed her up the steps to the courthouse.

Chapter Two

ᴔᴑ

God she wanted to kill the man. No wonder he couldn't keep a bookkeeper, he was a sadist in a Stetson. Who in the hell ever heard of a cowboy being a perfectionist? She'd been at the ranch two damned weeks, and in that time he'd complained about everything from her language to the way she dressed.

She had warned him she'd never kept books before, but he'd promised to teach her how. If she'd known exactly how little patience he had, she might have opted for the thirty days in jail. The man was a tyrant!

On the other hand, she'd not been able to hide her true feelings. Since the day he'd whipped her ass all those years ago for sneaking cigarettes, she'd been in love with him. Of course, it had started out as a young girl's crush before it blossomed into the first love of a teenager and now she was just head over heels and there wasn't a damned thing she could do about it.

Very frustrating, and to top it all off she knew she was making a pest of herself but couldn't seem to help it. When she was working, she would constantly go to him asking for help whether she needed it or not. Her need to be near him was a very real thing.

She was well aware that some of the ranch hands were whispering about her. *Well, let them whisper*, she thought not really caring what was said. Little did she know that the rest of the town was also speculating. The fact she conveniently ran into Hayden every chance she got, even when she wasn't working, made her fair game for local gossip.

Today though, all hell was going to break loose. She could feel the anger flowing off her body like molten lava and knew she'd be able to do nothing to hold it in check. He'd embarrassed her in front of half the ranch, and the only way she could keep from crying was to vent, which was exactly what she was doing when the door to the office was flung open.

The coffee cup shattered against the wall and in her anger, she didn't have time to fear the intimidating look that crossed his face.

"Don't say another word to me!" she screamed at him while looking for something else to throw.

"What in the hell is wrong with you, Austin?"

"Me? Wrong with me! You've got to be fucking kidding." Her hands were trembling with intense emotion, and she wasn't sure she'd be able to hold the tears back for long.

"You talk shit to me in front of the whole damned crew, and you think something is wrong with me?"

"I told you how it was going to be if you came to work for me and I meant it." His voice was steady and low in warning, but she was beyond caring.

"Yeah, you did," she said, her laugh bitter. "I've done what you've asked and tried my best to learn what you've taught, but I won't change who I am, not because you say so, Hayden O'Malley. You told me to change my clothes so I went home and changed, but that didn't seem to matter. I don't know what in the hell it is you want."

"I sent you home because your sorry excuse for underwear was riding up the back of your pants which were cut indecently low and your shirt didn't even meet the waist. You come back in painted-on jeans and a tank top small enough to fit a child. I won't send you home again, but you'll stay in the house for the remainder of the day, even through your lunch."

Austin wanted to curse him to the devil, but the black scowl on his face told her she wouldn't come out the winner so she kept her mouth closed. Turning her back on the infuriating man, Austin gave great effort to regaining her composure. It wasn't until the door to the office opened and then closed with a bang that she realized he was gone.

Quickly she cleaned up the shattered coffee mug she'd thrown in her fit of rage then sat at the desk and threw everything she had into her work.

Several hours had passed when she realized how cramped her muscles were and exactly how hungry she'd become. Making her way from the office, she approached the kitchen where she could hear muted voices. Not sure whether to interrupt or not, she slowed her pace, listening carefully. If the conversation seemed important, she would go back to the office, but if it was just some of the guys bullshitting, she would get herself something to eat.

After a moment, she recognized Hayden's voice, but she couldn't figure out who the other voice belonged to.

"That little filly's got herself all tied up over you, boss. The folks in town are wondering what you've got going on out here."

"She's just a kid with a crush, and I don't really care what the folks in town think."

Were they talking about her? Austin's heart began to race. Her palms became sweaty as she quietly inched closer to the door.

"I think she's got more than a crush, boss."

"Yeah, well that may be, but I'm not looking for a long-term woman. Besides, she's too young and not at all my type."

The words were like a blow to Austin's gut. She already knew she wasn't his type, but to hear him talk about her so dispassionately hurt. Maybe it was time to change, to up the ante a bit. Those were her thoughts as she returned to the office and jotted a short note for Hayden letting him know she was leaving early for the day.

Her mind spun with ideas on the drive back to town. Once back, her first stop was Claire's Thrift Shop. With not much money to spend, it was the only place Austin could think to go to buy some clothes. Clothes she hoped Hayden would find more to his liking.

She was extremely happy with her secondhand purchases when she left the shop, bags in tow, but through that happiness a gray cloud of doubt appeared.

She pushed it away and focused on tomorrow.

* * * * *

Had Austin stayed just a few more minutes she'd have gotten an earful. Hayden was so mad he could spit nails. Not sure why the conversation with one of his hands had turned angry, but it had and there wasn't a thing he could do about it now.

"Well boss, if you're not interested there are a few of us who are. Maybe we could keep Austin from throwing herself at you for the next couple of days at least." Before his employee had even finished the sentence, Hayden was seeing red. The thought of Austin allowing any of those fumbling idiots to put their hands on her made him want to kill.

"She's off-limits," he'd warned. "You be sure and tell the others."

With those words, he'd stormed from the kitchen to give Austin the same warning, only she wasn't there. In her place was a note. It made him wonder what in the world she was up to now and why he cared so much.

She hadn't been with him for long but she placed herself in his path every chance she got, leaving him ready. Every time he saw her lush body or smelled her sweet scent, he wanted to attack.

He had to remind himself several times a day that she was much too young for him. Yet at the same time, his cock reminded him that she was a grown woman who knew the score. Why shouldn't he be added to her list of conquests? If the rumor circulating through town was true, she was a mighty fine fuck.

The whole damned thing sucked as far as he was concerned and there had to be a way to stop it. To keep her away from him so his cock could return to normal instead of staying painfully erect throughout the day. He'd have to give it some thought, something would have to give and soon, or he was going to make a complete ass out of himself.

That night he was completely restless. Nothing he did seemed to help. Fresh air, warm milk, nothing. He was hard as steel and horny as hell to boot. He needed a woman but there wasn't one handy so he'd just have to take matters into his own hands. Literally.

Hayden rolled over until he was on his back, leaning against the headboard with several pillows behind him. One squirt from the bottle of lotion sitting on his bedside table prepared him. In the next instant, he wrapped his fist around the base of his jutting cock. It was nowhere near as good as the tight sheath of a wet cunt or as all-consuming as the heat of a humid mouth with full lips, but it would have to do.

He liked his women docile and willing. There was nothing better than a woman who could follow directions in the bedroom and take what he gave without complaint. It had been a while since he'd had full reign over that type of woman.

He believed beyond a shadow of a doubt he'd been born a century or two too late. There weren't many women left like that, just as there weren't many old-fashioned working cowboys left.

His hips arched involuntarily as his hand stroked the length of his sex. The whole time he was thinking of docile women he was picturing Austin in his head. If she wasn't the farthest thing from docile, he didn't know who was.

He could imagine the feel of her tiny hand working his flesh. She wouldn't be intimidated by his size and she wouldn't be inhibited by his needs. He could readily picture her tied to his bed belly down with pillows below her hips.

The position would thrust her hips back and up allowing him full access to her, to do with her as he pleased. He wondered which of her toys she liked the most? Did she use them often?

He'd heard she hosted a damned good party and passed out fliers to the women with each of the toys she sold, rated based on her and other clients' personal opinions. The woman was just too much.

There was a tingling sensation low in his spine warning him he was getting closer. Intensifying his grip, he increased his tempo. With a picture of Austin on her knees in front of him, he spewed his seed along his belly.

"Holy shit," he raged. The damned imp could get to him even when she wasn't around. He would have to do something to keep her from invading his thoughts. Something to ensure she stayed far from the heart he thought was protected so well.

* * * * *

The next morning came too soon for his liking. Little sleep and sexual frustration left him in a foul mood. The furrow plastered firmly between his brows should be enough to warn off even the most obtuse of people.

He was going over some newly received bills at the desk when she came into the room. He couldn't help it when his jaw dropped or seem to stop the flow of blood that, as usual in her presence, quickly flowed south. His cock stood at attention begging for a piece of the curvy little baggage sashaying toward the desk.

She looked so sweet. It was a ruse of course, because there wasn't a sweet bone in her body — she was mean through and through, and from the glittering look in her eyes, she knew exactly what she was doing.

Her blue eyes sparkled, he wasn't sure with what emotion, but it made her seem extremely happy. Her dimpled smile added to the effect. Lush lips were once again coated generously with peach gloss but he could tell she'd nibbled a bit at her bottom lip. He longed to be the next to nibble the delectable expanse of flesh.

Her hair was no longer blindingly red. Instead, it was the color of honey and made her look even younger. Instead of sticking up every which way in a mess of spikes, it looked as if it had been blown dry and was curled delicately around the edge of her cherubic face.

His mouth had gone dry, then wet at the difference in her appearance and he hadn't even made it to her body yet. If he wasn't careful, he might expire before he was done assessing her body.

Continuing his perusal, he let his eyes wander lower. The neckline of her dress showed just a hint of cleavage as it hugged her generous curves. It was pale blue, but he couldn't tell what the fabric was from where he was sitting.

The waist nipped in with a belt showed off her curvaceous waist and generous hips in a very flattering way. The hemline stopped just above her knees allowing him to see her smooth, tanned legs. The low backless sandals and the bubblegum pink polish adorning her toes complemented the outfit.

All in all, the outfit was absolutely stunning and made it so he wanted to fuck her now more than ever. In effect, it inflamed his already bad mood until he wanted to strike out.

She was driving him crazy with her curves and sass, and he would have to do something to push her away before she found herself underneath him in his bed, which was exactly where she would be if his cock had its way.

Chapter Three

✖

Austin wanted to shout in triumph at the look plastered across Hayden's face. It was as if he'd never seen a woman before. Or maybe he'd just never seen her dressed as a woman before.

She was well aware that her choice of clothing was offensive to some people. Especially living in Texas where it seemed most everyone was at least a generation behind. It was her style though, and she'd always done exactly what she wanted and planned to keep it that way.

She had to admit, even if it was only to herself, that it felt nice to dress the way she was dressed. She couldn't wait to try out a few of her other outfits just to see what type of reaction she'd get with them.

"See anything you like, cowboy?" she asked seductively as she walked toward him. She was a bit stunned when a string of curse words that burned even her ears flew from his pinched mouth.

It took him only a minute to stand from his seated position and storm from the room allowing the door to bang shut behind him.

"I won't cry, I refuse to cry," she whispered as the tears threatened to spill from her eyes.

She spent the rest of the day working at the computer until she was cross-eyed and her head ached, and still felt as if she hadn't accomplished a thing.

She had a party to host, and for the first time ever, she wasn't in the mood. As she made her way to the front door and was just about to open it, she heard a sound coming from behind her.

She knew it was Hayden before she saw him. The manly scent wafting around her as well as the sound of his clanking spurs on the hardwood floor told her what her body already knew.

Every hair on the back of her neck stood at attention, but she wouldn't let it all get to her. She refused to let the hurt invade her for the rest of the day. Tomorrow she would come to work, even though it was the weekend, and hope for the best. Hope that Hayden was in a better mood or at the very least that he wouldn't take his black mood out on her.

The pounding in her head grew worse by the minute. She hadn't eaten a bite of food or left the office for as much as a drink of water. She felt weak and sad and didn't want him to have any idea he could affect her so severely.

Squaring her shoulders, she turned to face him. "I'm leaving for the day, but I didn't finish, so I'll be back tomorrow. Goodnight, Hayden."

"Night," she heard him say in his slow Texas drawl as she slowly closed the heavy wooden door behind her.

What was going through his mind? He seemed so distant and cool. In a way, he'd always been that way but there were the times when he'd seemed caring and warm. The times when he'd looked at her as if she was a woman he'd want to be with, not only intimately but on an emotional and intellectual level.

There were certainly numerous times when she'd thought long and hard about what it would be like to be loved by him. He would be a possessive lover, one who wouldn't share.

Jealousy would be an issue with any woman he was with, as would trust. She'd heard stories of the one woman he had loved and how she had fucked him over. For the life of her, she couldn't fathom anyone screwing over such a fine man.

But if the stories she'd heard pertaining to Hayden and his ex-fiancée were true then he had every right to be a bit distrustful. However, he did not have the right to lump her in with all the women of loose morals just because she liked sex toys and was comfortable with her body.

Needing a bit of company, Austin picked up the phone and dialed the number for her new friend, Honor Rollings. It rang three times before she answered.

"Hello."

Austin wasn't sure if it was a good idea to invite Honor with her for the evening. Something told her Sean O'Malley wouldn't approve. On the other hand, he and Honor were only seeing each other, not actually married so what right did he have to say she couldn't go? A slight unease stayed with her before Honor's voice brought her out of her worried stupor.

"Hello? Is anybody there?"

"Hi, Honor, it's me, Austin. I know it's your night off. I could use a friend and was wondering if you'd like to help me host a party tonight?" She thought about her offer for a minute then added, "You can drive if you think it would be better that way." The legend of Austin and Jolene was well-known in the area. It was enough to make her snicker.

"Oh, that sounds like fun. What time would I need to be ready?"

Honor sounded excited and that surprised Austin into asking, "You don't think Sean will mind?"

"Oh, I didn't say that, but sometimes when things get just the slightest bit, regular, shall we say, I like to push my limits." Honor's voice had become husky and she gave an embarrassed giggle.

"All right, sweetie, if you're sure. I'll pick you up in an hour but be sure and leave a note because we won't be back until late. You might not mind the repercussions, but I think I might."

"No problem, Austin. See you in an hour."

The phone clicked in Austin's ear and although she still wasn't sure about taking Honor with her, it would be nice to have the company.

Honor Rollings was the type of woman you couldn't help but like. In the short time since they had been introduced, Honor had treated her with respect and Austin just knew they would end up lifelong friends.

The sensual party she hosted that night was just as big a hit as all the others. She brought one of just about everything in the catalog so the products could be looked at, touched and when it came to the lotions and such, tried. It was one of the reasons her parties were so popular. Honor's friendly presence and willingness to experiment helped the guests feel more comfortable.

The whole time she patiently answered questions, talked and took orders she thought of nothing but Hayden. She couldn't get him out of her mind. Naughty thoughts of him doing things to her she'd only dreamed of.

What would he taste like? Would his length feel hot against her lips? So many questions swirled through her mind and she wondered if she would ever get them answered firsthand.

She could picture a scene in her head where Hayden was making love to her. Her body arched as he kissed his way down until he reached her pussy. He fondled, nipped and licked at her until she thought she would go crazy. The whole time he talked dirty and instructed her on what to do. The sound of his lust-induced voice played like a broken record in the back of her head.

His voice would be rough and gravely as he gave explicit directions and she would follow them willingly to reach heights even the best toy couldn't bring about.

Her thoughts continued on the drive home. It felt as if she were crawling along the road. Jolene wasn't used to being driven at such a slow pace but Austin wanted in no way to further anger Judge Gumar or Hayden, so she followed the speed limit singing along to the radio and allowing her wicked thoughts full rein.

Honor's soothing voice kept her centered and although they sat in companionable silence most of the way, she was very glad Honor had agreed to go with her. From the look on Sean's face when they pulled into the drive at a quarter after one in the morning, Honor might not be so glad.

"Hi, Sean," she said trying to keep her unease at bay. There was just something about the O'Malley brothers that warned a woman not to show an ounce of fear.

"Hellion," he said before turning his hazel gaze to Honor. "In the house, darlin'. Me and you got some things to discuss."

Austin couldn't help the shiver that ran its course through her body at Sean's words. His voice was low, seductive and held promise. Honor was in big trouble. Turning toward her friend to apologize, Austin was surprised when Honor winked at her. When Austin felt Honor's arms engulf her and heard her friend whisper, "Don't worry, I know what I'm doing," the tension drained from her body.

Honor climbed from the low carriage of Jolene and was immediately gifted with a stinging swat to her backside. The loud *thwack* filled the still night air. "In the house, Little Darlin'," Sean commanded before stepping up to the driver's side window.

Austin couldn't help the blush that stained her cheeks as Honor rubbed her bottom, gave a saucy grin and turned toward the house.

"I hope you two behaved yourself, Hellion, because if you didn't you might be getting a bit of what Honor will be getting right now. Only you won't enjoy the effects quite as much, I'm sure." His words were in no way meant to be sensual but they caused her pussy to flood nonetheless. Would Hayden use a sound spanking as punishment? Would she like it? Something warned her that she would and that for her, it could easily become obsessive and go a bit deeper.

All or nothing was a motto she enjoyed in life. In this instance though, it was a scary proposition. One better left as a fantasy. One that couldn't become reality.

The next morning she awoke bleary-eyed but happy. It was a bright new day and she would make the best of it. She dressed carefully in the woven beige skirt and matching shirt she'd found for an unbelievably good price at Claire's, and did her hair once again in a softer and more sophisticated style. Adding simple gold hoops to her ears and a pair of dark brown pumps, she left her trailer for The Big O Ranch.

It was probably one of the funniest ranch names she'd ever heard and there were plenty of ranches in Texas to poke fun at, but the Big O had to take the cake. It was a sore spot for Hayden who refused to change the original name. He stated that it had been named the Big O Ranch by his ancestors, and as long as an O'Malley owned it, it would remain the Big O Ranch.

It was a subject Austin no longer brought up unless she was aiming for a fight. That thought flew from her mind as she opened the door to the office. Her heart dropped to her toes as she felt bile rise in her throat.

There on her knees in front of Hayden who sat just as proud as you please on the soft, oversized leather couch in the office, was Bunny Barnett. Aptly named, she was a tall, willowy blonde with less brains than a flea. Dressed in nothing more than a slinky black cocktail dress, which just happened to be gathered around her waist, Bunny showed off the bareness of her thong-clad ass. Austin wanted to throw up at the sight.

Evidently, brains weren't needed when it came to sucking dick because Bunny seemed to be doing a superb job of it, if the sound of Hayden's moans was any indication. Blinding anger combined with an overwhelming amount of jealousy stole over her, sweeping through every inch of muscle in her body.

Hayden's head was thrown back in ecstasy. If she had had a few emotion-free moments to think about it, Austin might have found the whole thing a bit funny. The way Hayden's jeans were sagging around his ankles, the tops of his boots barely showing over the white of his cotton boxer briefs. But there was no humor to be found.

Austin was so upset she shook with it and through the haze of red she had trouble remembering that Hayden had every right to do whatever he pleased, with whom he pleased in his own home.

She tried to quietly leave the room but in the process stumbled, causing her keys to clank against the door. She froze where she stood as Hayden looked up. Bunny stopped what she was doing, releasing Hayden's cock with a soft plop. She was about to rise when Hayden tightened his grip upon the back of her head. At the same time, he mumbled words for her ears alone causing her to resume her ministrations to his rigid cock.

Bunny's mumbled sounds of pleasure filled the room making Austin want to bash her over the head with the closest blunt object. Instead, she gathered every ounce of the strength inside of her and said, "I'm sorry. Please excuse me." The last came out on a ragged breath as she fled the room.

She'd just opened the door and bent her shaking knees to climb into Jolene when the front door opened. Bunny Barnett walked out as if nothing were amiss followed closely by Hayden who wore nothing more than a pair of jeans and his scuffed boots.

From the look of it, he was still proudly aroused. Briefly, she wondered what type of torture she could bestow upon the unfeeling asshole.

With trembling fingers, she started Jolene. She wanted to get the hell out of there before she was forced into an uncomfortable conversation with her boss, but luck wasn't on her side.

The look in her eyes made his chest ache and that scared the hell out of him. The way she tried to hide the pain made her look even more vulnerable. He longed to pull her into his arms, to ask for forgiveness, but he couldn't. To do so would lead to things neither of them was ready for. Instead, he would complete his plan effectively putting an end to any feelings she had for him. It was the only thing he could think to do.

After thanking Bunny for her help, he strode with a casualness he didn't feel to Austin's car. She was sitting as still as a stone statue, he felt like scum, but it was for her own good.

He saw her eyes move and knew damned well she'd seen him standing beside her car but she didn't budge. He tried to open the door but found it locked so he knocked on the driver's side window.

"Open up, Austin."

She did as he asked but continued to keep her eyes averted from him. "Now don't go acting all embarrassed, darlin', we both know you've been caught in the act, it's no different for me."

Her head snapped toward him, her eyes blazing. "It would be really hard for me to get caught in the act being a virgin and all," she said slowly, making sure he heard every word she spoke.

Her cheeks were red flags on her face, her anger and hurt was palpable, but he felt he had no choice but to continue. "Sure, sweet thang, whatever you say," he drawled in his most sarcastic tone.

Her chin wobbled with the effort not to cry. *Damn!* He swore under his breath. *Please don't let those tears fall,* he pleaded silently as he shoved his fisted hands into his pants pockets in order to keep from reaching for her.

Her words cut to the quick. "I don't know what I ever did to you, Hayden O'Malley," she started when he cut her off.

She knew exactly what she did to him sashaying that tight, little, barely covered ass in front of him day in and day out. She drove him nuts!

The little bit of anger her words brought to the forefront urged him on. Ruthlessly he spoke to her. "Don't act the shy little virgin with me, Austin, and don't pretend you haven't been following me around like a bitch in heat. In case you haven't noticed, you aren't even close to being my type."

All the color drained from her face leaving her skin sallow-looking, but the look of horror in her eyes was what made him feel like the bastard he was. *Just finish it already*, he thought, knowing by doing so he would never have another chance at anything more than a passing relationship with Austin Calhoun.

"The new clothes are real nice, darlin', but they don't make the woman."

He couldn't stand there a moment longer or he would pull her out the damned window and beg for forgiveness. Head high and what was left of his heart in his throat, he turned on his booted heel and strode angrily to the door.

Briefly, he paused on the lowest porch step then turned when he didn't hear her car leave.

"Take the rest of the weekend off Austin, I might just have more company later, but be here bright and early Monday morning or Judge Gumar and I might just find a reason to have lunch."

It was a threat he immediately regretted making when her car spit gravel as it skidded around the corner leading to the long dirt road she'd have to take before reaching the highway.

"Son of a bitch!" he swore as he headed in the house. He couldn't think of a single person to call to find out if she made it home okay so he prayed instead, and hoped that he hadn't just made the biggest mistake of his life.

The rest of the day was spent working tirelessly, trying to forget all that had happened just that morning. It had only been hours and yet it felt like days. He prayed with every shovelful of shit that she wouldn't call his bluff. He didn't know why but he had to see her again. Even though he'd purposefully hurt her and in no way wanted to, he cared for her.

The thought of Austin with another man, any man, was enough to make him spitting mad, and yet at the same time, he wouldn't accept her for himself. What kind of man was he?

The night was worse than all the others combined. Being horny and alone was one thing, but being downright miserable sucked. Instead of erotic dreams, he kept dreaming of the hurt in her big blue eyes as they swam with unshed tears.

The way she held herself still, barely breathing, and how pale her normally creamy skin had been. He'd caused the whole damned mess and some niggling thought in the back of his mind warned him that it would take a small miracle to turn around the events he'd just put in motion.

He was ashamed of the words he'd spoken to her. Never in his thirty-eight years had he chastised a woman for not being a virgin or for what she did behind closed doors. It was none of his business who did who, and he'd just gone and broken the one rule he'd always stuck to...

You don't stick your nose into other people's personal lives.

* * * * *

Sunday came, the day dreary and gray, just the way Hayden felt. After finishing his morning chores, he drove into town for a drink at O'Malley's and to visit his brother Sean.

The place was packed. It seemed like half the town was there to watch NASCAR on the big screen TV Sean was so proud of. Shouts and curses rang throughout the dimly lit room as several cars spun and crashed in a flurry of metal and rubber.

Hayden noticed several of the regulars kept sending quick glances his way. Instead of waiting, he asked Sean what was going on.

"Something I'm missing here?" he said, trying not to let his discomfort show.

Sean's meaty hands neatly folded the white bar towel he'd been using to dry beer mugs. "I'd say. You're the talk of town." Hayden groaned. He could only imagine what talk he was involved with this time.

"What this time?"

"Well, this time you are only indirectly involved. Seems most of the older men of the town—" he said, nodding toward a table of regulars "—thought you'd be the one to get Austin to behavin'. They were all just a bit surprised when she made a spectacle out of herself last night."

His body tensed with Sean's words. He shouldn't ask because it wasn't any of his business but he had to know. Knowing he'd regret asking the question before it was even out of his mouth didn't stop him from doing it.

"What did she do this time?"

"Aw, not much, really. She and a group of her girlfriends came in last night and had a bit too much to drink. There was a group of young bucks in here all fancied up in suits who seemed kind of smitten for a while there. They did some dancin' and just had a good time from what I can tell, but you know those old boys like to talk."

"She didn't drive herself home, did she?" If she did, he was going to wring her neck right after he whipped her ass.

"Damn, Hayden, what do you think I am? Of course she didn't drive herself home, Honor took her, but when I opened up this morning her car was already gone so I have no idea when she picked it up or who brought her here to get it."

Sean seemed to be thinking and then added, "Honor got herself a pretty red ass the other night after I came home from work and found a note that she'd gone to one of them parties with The Hellion. I gotta say, Hayden, I don't much care for Honor and Austin getting together."

Hayden took a long drink from his bottle of beer. "Sounds like your problem," he muttered as he laid some money on the smooth surface of the bar. He drove home wondering where Austin was and what she was doing.

Chapter Four

❧

It took the experience of a true woman and the know-how of a wanna-be makeup artist to get the purple smudges concealed beneath her red eyes. Sunglasses would have to do the rest.

The tears she'd shed last night would be the last. The time she'd been wasting on a man who cared nothing for her would be no more. She'd made a promise to herself and intended to keep it. It was the only thing that would help her through her six-month stint of service at the Big O Ranch.

With a wall firmly built around her tattered heart, Austin climbed into Jolene and made her way to work. It was a bright and sunny Monday morning and she planned to make the best of it. No matter how hard it was, she would not let Hayden O'Malley get the best of her nor would she let her traitorous body lead her astray. If she had to find a substitute for the rough and rugged rancher then she would.

At twenty-four it was time her virginity took a backseat and she learned what it was to truly be a woman. Watching not only the road, but also the flat land extending along both sides of the highway, Austin realized what a futile effort it would be to try and find a replacement for Hayden. He was a one of a kind man.

Disgusted with the road her thoughts had taken, she mentally braced herself for the confrontation to come. And it would come just as surely as the sun rose every morning. Out of sheer spitefulness, she'd worn another of her slightly used outfits.

The outfit might not make the woman, as Hayden so eloquently pointed out, but it sure made her feel womanly, so she tried with all her might not to give a shit what anyone else thought.

Of course, that all flew right out the window when she stopped off at the local diner for a fountain soda before heading off to the ranch. She'd run into none other than Bunny Barnett.

Damn! She swore under her breath. The gods must be really pissed at her for some reason.

"Well, if it isn't our very own little sex goddess," Bunny taunted, a malicious smile on her face.

Austin couldn't help the venom that dripped from her voice. "Funny coming from someone who was caught red-handed, or should I say lipped, with her mouth wrapped around O'Malley cock, wouldn't you say, Bunny?"

Austin knew it was petty but for once, she felt like lashing out at the label she'd been branded with, if they only knew. Bunny's next words were spoken with pure malice.

"Jealous, little girl?" Her next words were mortifying and said loud enough that the room at large heard. "Claire's must be having a sale or something." The evil witch laughed. "Saw that exact same outfit on Norma Lions just before she joined that diet club of hers. I'd heard she'd pawned all her fat clothes off at Claire's."

The twinkle in Bunny's eyes made Austin want to kill. In two steps, she was face-to-face with the simpering fool and ready to knock her block off. She'd just cocked her arm back and was ready to let it fly when two very large hands lifted her in the air then set her back down.

"Who in the fuck do you..." she got out before she noticed just who it was—Sean O'Malley and he didn't look happy.

"Uh-uh, Little One. I wouldn't go there if I were you." His eyes were angry and his mouth wasn't smiling.

She knew she'd not be getting a hold of Bunny Barnett today so she turned to Sean with her head held high and said with as much dignity as possible, "Thanks, Sean, you probably just saved my ass from Judge Gumar."

She was just making her way to the door when Bunny hollered out, "Just like your clothes, Austin, leftovers are all you'll ever get when it comes to men."

"Not if I can help it," she mumbled as she let the door close behind her without bothering to look back.

She replayed their conversation over in her head several times before she turned Jolene's steering wheel sharply, flipping a shitty right there on the highway, and made her way back home to change.

From now on, she was going to be herself no matter who it angered. The trip to the ranch after her harrowing confrontation with Bunny was shrouded in insecurities she wouldn't allow to bring her down.

With a fake-as-hell smile welded to her pale face, Austin entered the sprawling ranch house. It was like coming home, minus the warm welcome. The place itself called to her, warming her from the inside out. The heavy wooden door was illuminated by the sunlight as it filtered through the beautifully worked stained glass surrounding it on both sides.

The wood floor of the foyer was gently worn from years of work boots and spurs scuffing its surface. She liked the way it sounded beneath her sandal-clad feet. Making her way to the kitchen, she warmly greeted the men who stood about sipping coffee and eating hotcakes fresh from the griddle.

With practiced ease, she spared a glance for Hayden. "Mr. O'Malley," she said in way of greeting hoping her smile seemed genuine and not at all like the grimace she felt it was.

His eyes narrowed in suspicion, their hazel depths staring intensely as though they could see right through her.

Her nipples peaked beneath the thin surface of her lace demi-cup bra. She was sure they were visibly noticeable through the thin stretch cotton of her black ribbed tank top.

She'd worn it on purpose because she knew Hayden absolutely hated it.

Black with the stark picture of a white trailer right in the center when read properly, it would amount to *White Trailer Trash*. It was sort of an inside joke between herself and her three closest friends. Over the years, they'd all lived in a trailer at some point in time. Only she and one other could be classified as butt-white so they threw the jab back and forth. A bit of friendly banter between friends who were close enough to be sisters. Just another little glitch to show off her less-than-normal sense of humor. It was too bad none of them lived close by—she sure could use a shoulder right about now.

For some reason though, Hayden found it offensive and told her so whenever he saw her wearing it. He also seemed to complain nonstop about her choice of living accommodations as if he had every right to do so.

The more she thought about the blithering idiot, the more she thought she was probably a hell of a lot better off without his possessive, overbearing ways cluttering up her life. Then her heart would ache, accompanied by the sting of unshed tears. Then she'd mourn for what was never meant to be.

She looked absolutely horrible and it was all his fault. His emotions were raw, torn, leaving him feeling as if he'd just climbed aboard the world's longest roller coaster with an open-ended ticket.

"Austin," he spoke carefully. The effort it took to keep his voice modulated, to keep himself from pulling her into his arms was overwhelming in its intensity.

Her eyes skittered from his, but he could see the rapid rise and fall of her chest. Did the rest of the men notice how her pouty nipples pushed so erotically against the thin scrap of fabric she called a shirt?

Of course they did. That was her plan, to show him who was boss and today, right this minute, she'd get away with it because the last thing he wanted to do was break the fragile grasp she had on her control.

He could see it in every line of her too-young face. The way she held herself stock-still as if trying to sense the slightest change in the atmosphere around her. It would do no good to reprimand or confront her in front of the others, or alone, for that matter.

Today the only thing it would amount to would be hurt feelings and possibly even tears, and that wasn't something he was willing to deal with right now. It was hard enough to watch her gather her strength around her like a shroud.

When she changed from being as still as a day without so much as a breeze, to fluttering around the kitchen like a butterfly, he thought he would lose it. It was more her normal way to go about things, but the slight trembling in her fingers, as she gripped the coffeepot to fill her cup, told him all was not well.

Her movements were jerky and unproductive. It seemed as if she was running in circles and going nowhere fast. The woman was just plain ole jittery, always twitching about. It was enough to make a man nervous if he was inclined to nervousness.

Evidently the majority of his ranch hands were, because they cleared the kitchen as if they'd been called to bed by a longhaired vixen. Austin looked around the kitchen as if surprised to see it empty of bodies then mumbled an excuse and exited the room.

Hayden couldn't help but follow her. Part of him hoped she'd get back into that long monster she lovingly called Jolene and leave the ranch and never return. Another part of him was making sure she didn't do anything of the sort.

That stubborn, mule-headed part of him would tie her down if necessary to keep her on his land, within his grasp, right where she belonged. Too bad his separate sides couldn't get together and work out some sort of compromise, because he felt not only as if he was being ripped in two, but as if he would go fucking nuts in an extremely short amount of time if something didn't happen.

He stood at the partially open door and just watched for a few minutes. Watched the graceful way she prepared for the work ahead of her—even when it seemed as if she moved automatically, with no thought to her actions.

It seemed as if the life had been sucked from her. Her eyes no longer twinkled merrily and she wasn't humming any of her favorite country songs like she normally did. He missed the sound of her voice as the tune floated from her closed lips.

As if sensing his eyes upon her, her fingers halted over the keyboard just before she turned to him. The smile that crossed her lips barely curved the tips and didn't come even close to crinkling the corner of her eyes the way he was used to.

Her voice was nothing more than professional when she asked, "Is there something I can do for you, Mr. O'Malley?"

He had plenty of answers for the loaded question, but didn't voice a single one. The use of his last name bothered him but she knew damned well it would, which was why she was using it. He wouldn't be emotionally blackmailed to apologize or admit to feelings he wasn't ready for so he shook his head and stalked from the doorway.

The next two weeks passed by without much change. Some days seemed to fly by while others seemed to dawdle along like an old lady scurrying about with her britches around her ankles.

He was admittedly surprised when his father showed up at the Big O bright and early one morning.

"Damn, son, you've got this place looking grand." The compliment caused Hayden to slow his walk. Surprise and suspicion must have shown on his face. His father Collin O'Malley hooted with laughter, slapped him briskly on the back and said, "Don't look at me like that—just because I didn't care to have the place for myself doesn't mean I don't wish you the best."

More surprise. Hayden felt like he was in an episode of the *Twilight Zone*.

"Hear from Zane lately?"

"Not in a day or so, why?" More suspicion. Hayden wanted to warn the old man not to start on Zane the minute he came home, but the lecture wouldn't have been necessary. "Zane and his fiancée should be here sometime next week. Sure is going to be good to have him home."

"It's going to be wonderful to have my boys back together." Hayden couldn't help the cynical look he gave his father. Years of disappointment spurred him on. His father's next words sent his emotions tailspinning out of control.

"I know now that I was wrong. I'll say as much to your brothers, too. I'm proud of all three of you and can only ask that you forgive an old man for trying to run your lives."

Whew! Hayden thought, a bit startled. Never in a million years could he have imagined what it would feel like to hear those words.

Hayden had just released his father from a long-overdue embrace when Austin's boat of a car made its slow trek up the graveled road.

He couldn't seem to pry his eyes from her petite yet extremely curvy frame as she walked from her car to the house.

Her jeans were so tight she had to have had help getting them on, and her white shirt showed just the hint of a colored bra beneath. He'd have to get closer to see just what color the scrap of fabric was.

"You ever gonna claim that filly or just mess with her until you've broken her spirit?" That fast his mood went from shine to shit.

"She's driving me crazy. The damned woman is too stubborn for her own good. She won't even look my way

46

unless I address her personally. For Christ's sake, she calls me Mr. O'Malley."

His dad didn't sound too sympathetic. "From the talk in town, you've earned whatever she dishes out."

Hayden could feel his temper slipping a notch. "And just how do you figure that?" he demanded of the older man standing beside him—a man with hazel eyes identical to his.

"Well now, I don't even know where to start. From what Sean told me, he was in the diner when Bunny and Austin got into it pretty good."

"What?"

"Guess it got pretty ugly. Sean said that Austin was just about to knock Bunny down a peg when he intervened."

Hayden couldn't seem to form a coherent string of words but he had to know. "What was said?" he asked, wondering if he really wanted to know.

"The town, or at least those eating breakfast, got an earful about Bunny's lips and your cock."

Hayden couldn't help the strangled sound that escaped his throat but his father who didn't seem to notice continued.

"Sean said Austin was all gussied up in clothes a lot more suited to a woman with her attributes than what she had on just now," he said nodding to the door then continued. "Bunny made some comment about her secondhand clothes, called her fat and told her that just like clothes, she'd only ever get leftovers when it came to men. Yep, guess that about sums it all up." His father chuckled.

"Goddammit!" he roared, wanting to throttle Bunny, mentally kicking his own ass in the process. "She looks lost and like I said before, she won't even talk to me."

"Isn't that what you wanted, son?"

"I thought it was but I don't know what in the hell I want anymore." That was a lie. He wanted to hold and soothe her flesh-to-flesh after he ate every inch of her, forcing orgasm after orgasm from her taut body. "She's too young, Dad. You know how I am. In a matter of months in my care, she'd be begging me to let her leave and I wouldn't be able to do it. Once I have her, I'll never let her go."

"Tell her as much, Hayden," Collin O'Malley said, laying a comforting hand on Hayden's shoulder.

Hayden couldn't get the conversation with his father out of his mind. Good advice all around, but could he follow it? Should he follow it? He spent the next few days watching Austin. Trying to figure out what in the hell he should do.

She continued about her daily business as if nothing was amiss. Except for the fact that she'd lost weight, her color was pale and her eyes listless, she acted as if nothing was wrong. No one else seemed to notice, but he had. Every new frown line, every red-eyed morning struck him in the most uncomfortable way.

The fact she'd taken to staying out late at night partying with friends should be none of his business. The calls he'd received telling of her latest daredevil antics shouldn't have made his heart leap into his throat, but no matter how much he tried to deny it to himself, he was worried about her.

Her continuance in addressing him by his last name was growing old and his last nerve was getting mighty frazzled. If she didn't straighten her ass out, he was going to paddle it good and proper. The only problem was, once he got his hands on her, he might never let her go.

Storming into the office this morning probably hadn't been the best thing to do, but he wanted to throttle someone and she had been handy. Besides, it was her actions that had riled him in the first place.

Chapter Five

ॐ

"What has gotten into you, Hellion?" he'd thundered, his voice rising above the tune playing softly from the radio.

She jumped but said nothing. Instead, she turned from him giving him her back as if he didn't exist. When he felt like he was going to explode, his anger so strong, he stalked to the desk and stopped her fingers by grasping them tightly in his hands.

"Let go," was all she said. Her voice was cold and hard, nothing like the happy, sensuous woman he thought he knew so well.

"I was just told that you and a group of your *friends* —" he sneered the word as if it left a bitter taste in his mouth then continued " — parked out in my pasture and went swimming in my pond."

He wanted for her to deny it, to vow that she'd not done such a thing with other men. Instead, she turned to him, her blue eyes like lasers as they bored into him with wickedness as if sizing him up.

"I don't know where you got your news, Hayden, but someone is sadly mistaken." His sigh was audible in the quiet of the room but his relief was shattered when she opened her mouth and demolished the tenuous thread he held on his legendary O'Malley temper.

"There wasn't much swimming involved. Plenty of drinking and even a bit of skinny-dipping, but nope, not much swimming." The laugh tinkling from her mouth was cut off when he jerked her to her feet.

The only thing stopping her forward motion was his broad chest. Hayden left her no time to utter a word before crushing his mouth to hers. Her taste was exotic, warm and dark, with a promise of more.

The ferocity of his kiss increased as he thought of her lush body naked for others to view. It made him sick with jealousy. Mind-numbing arousal spurned forth by anger left him out of control. There was no telling what might have happened if someone hadn't knocked at the door.

The loud rapping sound brought him out of his fit of rage and jealousy to frantic hands pushing at his chest. Her face was ghostly pale, all except for the small dot of crimson on her lower lip. With the tip of his tongue, he wet his own tasting her blood in the process.

Every ounce of anger in him drained away in that instant only to be filled with dread and shame.

"Oh, God, darlin'," he groaned, taking a step toward her stopping quickly when she retreated. He wanted to shout at the heavens, to roar with the grief of what he'd almost done.

"Boss," a voice called from the hallway just outside the door.

"What is it?" he snapped, never once taking his eyes from Austin. His hazel orbs followed her movements as she wiped the tiny speck of blood from her lip using the back of her hand. She wiped as if to remove any remnant of him from her person.

With trembling hands, she applied a generous amount of lip gloss and sat back at the desk as if nothing had happened.

"There's a problem with the new foal. I wanted you to have a look before we call out the vet."

Damned ranch business, he thought but answered, "I'll be right there."

Moving closer to the desk his eyes narrowed as her whole body stiffened.

"Goddammit to hell, Austin! You know I won't hurt you." When she said nothing he strode to the door and jerked it open.

She said something low. It drifted to his ears on a whisper and tore at his heart. "You already have."

"This isn't over, Hellion. Not by a long shot." With those ominous words, he left the office and the house, slamming both doors behind him on his way out.

His body ached from the way her curves had molded against him. The feel of her breasts mashed against his chest as he'd lifted her to her tiptoes made him wonder what the swells of flesh would taste like.

Would her nipples be rose-tipped or darker and large? He allowed his thoughts to wander before reeling them in tightly to deal with the sick foal. It would be hours before he could get away from the stables. Hours in which Austin would have time to regain her composure, but would that serve to work against him or for him?

He wouldn't know until the next time he saw her, talked to her, and that bothered him. It bothered him even more when he was finally able to make his way back to the house only to find her gone.

No note, nothing. His patience was running on low if their encounter in his office was any indication, and he feared when it finally snapped, they would both pay. He'd never do anything to physically hurt her, but if she kept pushing his limits, testing her boundaries, she would soon find out that there was no way out.

Once he claimed her, there would be no going back. He desperately needed to talk to her before he did something really stupid like take her to his bed then refuse to let her go.

He'd go into town this evening and stop by the pub. He needed to talk with Sean anyway, he'd kill two birds with one stone because before leaving town he planned to stop off and talk with Austin, to do as his dad suggested then let her make her own decision.

With a decision firmly in place, he headed off to shower and jack-off, he'd need all the help staying in control he could get.

* * * * *

It was Friday night and Austin couldn't think of a thing to do so when a friend came by her tiny trailer and offered her a ride to O'Malley's Pub for some drinks, Austin quickly agreed.

Leaving Jolene at home wasn't something she liked to do, but it would be safer, especially since she'd already had two run-ins with Sean O'Malley. She wasn't at all sure if he abided by a three-strike rule, and decided it would be safest not to test the overly large man.

The boisterous crowd she was with enjoyed every minute of the fun they were having.

"So Austin, they tell me you've got a naughty little side business going." The man who spoke behind her was as light as Hayden was dark. Handsome wasn't a word she would use when describing him, he was pretty. As pretty as a man could get and still look the least bit masculine.

If he's so pretty, why doesn't he make you feel the way Hayden does? Her inner voice taunted her.

Just thinking about Hayden's commanding presence made her pussy flood. Tiny spasms ran the length of her inner muscles driving her crazy with need, the ripples strengthening as she thought about how roughly he had handled her earlier in the day.

If only she could tell him how it had excited her even while she'd been frightened. There was so much she didn't know, wanted to learn, if only he'd give her the chance.

No! He doesn't want you, so get over him. She wished it wasn't true, but unfortunately it was.

She'd seen Hayden walk in. He hadn't paid any attention to their table, which was probably for the best. Her hair was in its usual disarray and highlighted with burgundy. The color complimented the spaghetti-strapped denim dress she wore.

The man still standing behind her pulled her chair back from the table with her still firmly seated in it causing Austin to giggle like a schoolgirl. When he motioned for her to get up, she did so without much thought. Tonight she was just out to have a good time. To forget all that had happened during the past week and enjoy herself.

"I'm Bill. I don't think we've been properly introduced," he said, grasping her hand firmly within his. Austin watched as he raised her hand to his lips and kissed her knuckles sensuously before sitting in her chair.

Before she could make a comment about his rudeness, he plunked her down onto his lap. His erection was evident beneath her ass, causing her to still.

He gave a breathy chuckle then said in her ear, "Don't worry, sweetheart, I can control him."

Austin felt instantly at ease and laughed with Bill leaving the others to wonder what had been said. She was still looking into Bill's face and laughing when the crowd around her grew ominously quiet.

Across the table from her, Hayden stood, his face a mask of black fury, white-knuckled hands dangling at his sides.

"Hellion, I think it's time you went home." His obnoxious behavior was beyond belief, and she wasn't going to put up with it. She stayed right where she was, not moving a muscle.

Bill's body tensed beneath her when Hayden strolled in his long-legged cowboy way around the table. It only took one look in his furious eyes for Bill to get the message.

Standing, he lifted Austin with him. Once he was sure she was steady on her feet, he took a step back from her as if handing her over.

"Are all men fucking Neanderthals?" she asked of no one in particular. She was getting really tired of being treated like a slab of meat.

Hands on her hips, one hip cocked precariously to the side, Austin narrowed her eyes at Hayden. "You made your opinion of me crystal clear, Mr. O'Malley. Now if you don't mind, I'm trying to have fun with a few friends," she said then prepared to sink back into her seat.

Only that didn't seem to be what Hayden had in mind. He was so quick she didn't have time to make a run for it or to fight him in any way.

"Too many friends for my comfort, Hellion," he growled before he tossed her over his shoulder. She was no lightweight and for a moment, her evilly vicious side hoped the asshole would throw his back out.

"Dammit to hell, Hayden O'Malley! You'd better put me down before I kick your cowboy ass all over Texas."

A loud whack filled her ears just before a burning sensation spread across her bottom. In morbid fascination, her pussy soaked the thin fabric of her panties. She could feel it coating her inner thighs and wondered if Hayden could smell her arousal.

"Ouch! You son of a bitch," she yelled, earning herself another blistering swat.

"Shut up, Austin, before I give you a real good reason to curse," he growled, his voice a low rumble warning her of his lack of control.

All she could see in her upside down position as she was hauled out of the pub was a nervous Honor and a widely smiling Sean. Goddamned O'Malley men and their wicked ways.

Hayden was either a cowboy with more behind his fly than under his hat or had more balls than the local football team. Austin wasn't sure which.

First he acted like he wanted her working for him then he became an impatient tyrant. He openly humiliated her and kept her away and then when she stayed away, he carries her off into the night like a caveman claiming his woman.

The damned idiot changes his mind more than an old woman, she mused silently.

Then it struck her. Like a lightning bolt to the heart, it finally dawned on her.

Maybe he finally realized he loves me.

Her heart hammered against her chest. The feeling made her dizzy. Lightheadedness seemed to flow over her, taking every coherent thought with it. She didn't even think to ask why Hayden was taking her to the Big O instead of home.

Chapter Six

✑

"It's over, Hellion. I've tried everything to stay away from you, but you just wouldn't listen." It didn't seem as though she was listening now, but he continued anyway.

"You just keep pushing and pushing. Well, you've won, or lost. I guess it all depends on your point of view." That seemed to get her attention.

He was so damned angry at the way she was flirting, rubbing herself all up on pretty boy that he wanted to bare her ass and take his belt to her. Instead, he lectured and scolded, hoping she would come to understand the magnitude of what was happening.

"I tried to save you your carefree existence," he started, but was cut off.

"By hovering over me and telling me what to do all the fucking time!"

"Watch it, little girl. You wanted me, well now you've got me. Just remember. Not only did you get an older man but you got a possessive, domineering older man and I don't intend to change."

He was well aware of his faults, had been reminded of them often over the years. All that no longer mattered. There was something about Austin Calhoun that drove him crazy.

No matter how hard he tried, he just couldn't understand it. She cursed like a truck driver with that big mouth of hers and was obnoxious as all get out. At the same time he wanted to wash her dirty mouth out with soap, he also wanted to see it, feel it wrapped tightly around his cock, draining it until it was flaccid and in need of rest.

And when it was good and rested, he wanted to fuck her every way he could think of until she begged for mercy, until her body glistened damply with perspiration.

She continued to stare out the side window as if in a daze. The mulish look on her face warned him her mind was whirling and she was pissed. The stubborn jut of her chin warned of problems ahead.

As his truck crunched through the gravel of the driveway, she moved subtly as if not to draw attention to herself. Her rounded body was as stiff as a steel rod, one hand gripping the armrest tightly. Her fingers grazing the door handle.

"Touch that handle when I stop this truck and there'll be hell to pay." There was no way he was going to chase her down like a wayward calf bawling for its mama.

Her blue eyes snapped to his, narrowed and intent, but she said nothing in return.

After putting the truck in park Hayden removed the keys from the ignition, climbed from the cab and walked around where with the help of a hand on her elbow, he helped Austin out of the vehicle.

He wanted to soothe her—to assure her all was just fine but he wasn't in the soothing mood and he wasn't too damned sure things would ever be okay again.

There was definitely something going on between the two of them, something he wasn't yet ready to deal with. For now, he was going to get a taste of what she'd been teasing him with. It could go one of two ways.

That single taste could set him free or addict him for life. Either way, it was going to happen. He would deal with the consequences when the time came.

In the foyer, he backed Austin against the now closed door. His mouth swooped down upon hers in a kiss that blindingly consumed him.

"Open up for me," he murmured against her lips.

They were soft and plump, just like the rest of her, and they tasted like peaches, all sweet and tangy. He absently wondered if her juicy nether lips would taste the same way.

"Hayden," she panted when his lips finally released hers. "Oh, Hayden."

Her voice sounded breathless and weak, bringing out the protective beast within him. He tried not to think of how loving it was to hear his name all breathy on her lips.

Her chest heaved with the effort to breathe. Her breasts swayed with the movement, tantalizing his senses.

For years, he'd wondered what she would look like. His large hands ached to caress each swell, to pluck and pinch at her nipples until they were distended and ultra-sensitive, until she moaned and screamed in frustration. Then he would suckle them deep into his mouth and torture each globe with tongue and teeth making her come without even a touch to her pussy.

To see his dark hands against her pale full breasts would be like heaven.

Abruptly he released her. Her body sagged against the wall as if she was powerless to move. He'd help her if need be. Right now, no excuse would be enough to release her. Unless she told him no, he wasn't going to relent.

"Upstairs. My room. Now." That was about all he could get out as his cock swelled and pulsed against the confining fit of his jeans.

When she didn't move fast enough, he placed a hand at the small of her back as if to propel her forward, but there was no need.

His eyes became feral as Austin turned to him causing him to stop in the center of the hall. He growled his frustration trying to move her along.

His cock was dying for attention. If he didn't sink every inch of his shaft into her at the earliest possible moment, he would go insane.

When her small hands fumbled with his zipper as she tugged him forward, he relaxed a bit. She walked backwards while she worked his pants, completing the task of freeing his engorged sex just as they reached the door.

"I want you in my mouth, Hayden." Her words were husky and if he didn't know better, he'd think she sounded hesitant.

His answer to her question was to thrust her into the room, slamming the door behind them. He lowered his lengthy frame into the cozy chair in the corner of the spacious room then beckoned her.

"Right here, darlin'. Bring that sweet mouth of yours over here. I want your face buried in my lap taking all of me, Austin. All of me."

Her pupils were dilated, her cheeks flushed and she stumbled a bit as she made her way to where he sat. She licked her lips just before dropping to her knees. The seductive movement made his shaft bob in welcome, a single drop of liquid dribbled from its tip.

On her knees in front of him, she looked up until their eyes met. She said nothing before lowering her head, taking him in the moist cavern of her mouth until he was seated within her all the way to the root.

"Holy hell," he cursed, the feeling exquisite.

Holy hell just about said it all, Austin thought, as she tasted Hayden. His scent was spice and musk and his pubic hair tickled her nose making it twitch.

"Mmmmm," she couldn't help but hum in appreciation of the generous length and width of his cock as she lifted her head, running her tongue around the bulbous head along the way.

Technically she was a virgin, and as a virgin, the thought of taking him completely within the depth of her body made her a bit nervous.

59

Out of all of her toys, none were as large or as big around as the real thing she held in her mouth. Just the thought of it made her tremble, probably with a combination of fear and anticipation.

Anticipation seemed to be winning out, if the slick juices she could feel coating her inner thighs were any indication.

Although she felt a bit embarrassed by it all, she was so aroused it didn't matter that the sounds of her slurping at his rigid flesh filled the room.

His taste and texture was so new, so consuming, that she thought she might come from giving him a blowjob. Needing the release, she decided to help herself along.

With one hand, she continued to hold the base of his cock. The other she trailed down the curve of her belly, widening her knees before she reached her pussy.

"I don't think so, Hellion," Hayden said.

He leaned forward dislodging his cock from her lips and grasped her wrist before she reached her soaked panties.

"Let go," she moaned.

"Not on your life, darlin'. As long as I'm here, willing and able, I'll do that. Unless I tell you otherwise."

Did he ever stop? She had been almost ready to come from blowing him, and he was still completely coherent. It wasn't fair.

"Then do something, cowboy, I ache all over." Austin couldn't help the huskiness that wove itself through her voice. Her body was afire and he was the only one who could douse the flame.

His work-roughened hands pulled her to his lap where he stroked her inch by curvy inch. For a brief second, she was embarrassed at the thought of being naked in front of such a fine specimen of a man.

He was tall and muscular where she was short and plump. She only allowed the feeling to linger for a short time before she shook it off.

She was all woman, every inch of her size-twelve self and proud as hell of the fact. There were plenty of men out there attracted to curvy women. Austin knew it to be fact.

His fingers continued on an erotic journey up her thigh until they were tickling and tantalizing the spot where thigh and groin met. It was enough to cause her hips to arch as if begging for more.

Her mouth had no qualms about doing so. "It's time, Hayden. Oh, God, please." It wasn't like her to beg, but she was so ready she thought she might implode if she didn't explode into a thousand shards of bright light all over the room.

With two firm hands upon her waist, he lifted her, allowing him to stand. His lips claimed hers, making stars dance before her eyes.

He was so good with his mouth she didn't even notice he had moved them to the bed. Before she knew it, she was flat on her back with Hayden draped half on and half off of her. Her panties were gone and her dress was bunched around her waist.

The main thought to go through her mind while her body was being seduced into a frenzy was, *I can't believe he loves me.*

His fingers rubbed and plucked at her nipples through the denim of her dress. When he grew tired of fighting the fabric, he gave a single, swift yank to the neckline, scattering buttons everywhere. It was thrilling to be wanted so badly, and her breasts felt the same way. Their already large peaks seemed to swell, becoming even more sensitive.

The moment he stilled, she knew he'd spotted them. Two silver bars, each one running horizontally through a nipple.

"Dear God," he hissed, the air rushing over the sensitive peaks, wringing a moan from the back of her throat. "What do

I do with them?" he asked, a look of uncertainty in his eyes as if he was not at all sure of how to proceed.

Austin couldn't help but giggle then looking him in the eye she said, "Play with them, Hayden, suck them, love them. You won't hurt me, I promise."

Her words seemed to be enough. His mouth widened in an attempt to take in as much of her as possible. His teeth scraped her tender flesh sending a bolt of desire straight to her core.

"What are you waiting for, cowboy? Fuck me already." It was now or never and if he kept up with the torture, she thought it might just kill her. His next words almost did.

Of course, like the saying goes, all good things must come to an end. It seemed she was included in the equation and it hurt more than she could ever imagine.

To go from bliss to shit so fast was the last straw. He'd just finished fumbling in his jeans pocket, the sound of tearing foil grated on each sensually exposed nerve. Next time she would put the condom on him, with her mouth. It was something she'd read about and longed to try only after being doused with such humiliating words, she realized there wouldn't be a next time.

"I'm not waiting for a thing," he muttered, fumbling with the front of his jeans, lowering them a bit more. "It doesn't matter who you've been with as long as it's me you're with now."

His words stung more than a slap to the face but it was too late. No sooner had they left his mouth then she felt the velvety tip of his penis at her entrance.

"No," she moaned as he thrust into her with lust-driven intensity, seating himself to the hilt, her cry of pain filling the room around them.

Her body clenched causing more than just discomfort. She did all she could to hide it but failed miserably if Hayden's ruddy cheeks and disbelieving eyes were any indication.

"Son-of-a-mother-fucking-bitch!"

If she hadn't felt as though she were being split in two, she would have laughed at his out-of-character outburst, but her insides burned almost as much as her heart ached, and she couldn't seem to hold the tears at bay.

If this was what sex with a man was like, she'd just stick to toys.

Chapter Seven

ॐ

His mind screamed for him to get off of her but his body wouldn't obey. Her virgin tightness gripped his cock in a fist-tight grasp, and he realized with horror exactly what he'd done.

He wanted to lay blame, but there was nowhere for it to go. It was his alone. She'd told him she was a virgin and he'd laughed at her.

"If I ever get my hands on whoever started those rumors, I'll kill 'em," he mumbled.

Her trembling hands continued to push at his chest, her wriggling body sending him deeper into the abyss.

"Stay still, dammit!"

Her wide blue eyes streaked with tears stared at him from her pale face, a face that somehow seemed so different than it had moments ago. An innocent face he should not have taken for granted.

Bracing his weight on one arm, he tenderly wiped the tears from her cheeks being careful not to move. Hell, he was afraid to even breathe.

"Okay now?" he asked when he felt her body relax around his jutting cock.

She spoke not a word, only nodded her answer. He wasn't at all sure what to do now, so he decided to do what he should have done in the first damned place. Ask.

"Austin darlin', tell me what you want, what you need." He was hoping she would want to continue but wasn't going to hold his breath on it.

"C-could you get off me? O-out of me, Hayden, you're hurting me."

It was the last thing he wanted to do but at this point, he would have painted the moon blue had she asked. Her petite frame would have struggled to take him had she been experienced—he should have realized that in his lust-induced stupor.

The fact she had been a virgin only made matters worse. He knew she played around with sex toys, she wasn't shy about admitting it, but this was something completely different.

"Sure thing, sweetheart," he answered, stroking her short hair back at the bangs. "Take a breath and relax."

When she did as he asked, he slowly pulled his still-hard shaft from the tight clasp of her body, regretting the action instantly. Her breath hitched as the wide head of his cock slipped past the tight ring of her entrance. The movement caused her to wince.

He already missed the warmth of her and wasn't at all sure he would ever have such an opportunity again. Needing to make amends for his stupidity, he rose from the bed after kissing her tenderly on the lips.

"Stay right there, darlin'. I'll be right back."

He watched as she scooted up the bed toward the headboard trying to put what was left of her dress to rights along the way.

After knowing her for years, he could easily read the need to flee his presence in her crystal-blue eyes. Pinning her with a look, he strode with purpose to the bathroom pausing only long enough to say, "I mean it, Hellion. Now is not a good time to test me."

He was relieved to see her eyes narrow as they zoned in on him, replacing the lost look that had been haunting her features.

She probably wouldn't appreciate what he had in mind to do, might even be embarrassed after all that had just happened between the two of them, but it was the only thing he could think to do right now and come hell or high water, he was going to do it.

With a washbasin in hand and a fluffy, dry towel flung over his shoulder, he made his way back into the room. Her eyes were closed but she was far from asleep.

She'd covered herself with the colorful afghan he kept at the foot of the bed and although her eyes were closed as if in slumber, her body was as stiff as a board, her breathing erratic.

"Sit up, Austin," he said in a controlled voice. He meant business, but would be tender if it killed him. There was no way rough-and-tumble sex was going to be happening today or anytime soon for that matter if the stubborn angle of Austin's chin was any indication.

When he braced a knee on the side of the bed, her startled eyes flew open and her hands clutched the afghan like a shield.

"Up," he repeated, even as he helped her accomplish the task with an arm behind her.

"Why? I just want to go home, Hayden."

"Not yet." Not until he knew he'd given her good memories to replace the ones he'd so carelessly created.

"I'm fine. Really. I think we should just forget this ever happened. I'll stick with my toys, and you stick with women who know what fucking is all about. Simple."

The damned little idiot could test the patience of Christ himself, Hayden thought angrily.

"Listen and listen good, Hellion. I don't mind the toys. When you're alone have at 'em, it won't bother me at all, but if I'm around and able, you'd better come to me and not something operated by batteries. We can use them together. Got it?"

He knew it wasn't even close to being the right time to discuss the subject, but the thought of her with a buzzing contraption probing her secret places when his cock could be doing the same, pissed him off royally.

Her cheeks flushed instantly as she jackknifed on the bed sitting as straight as a board.

"Fuck off, Hayden. You've got no say in the matter. I'll play with myself anytime I damned well please and there isn't a thing you can do about it. You got that?" she sneered the words at him.

He wanted to shake her or paddle her or both, but now wasn't the time. There would be a time and a place for this particular battle just as all the others. For now, he would let it go.

Instead of arguing with her, he leaned into her body and kissed her. She stiffened but didn't pull away, leaving him with a bit of hope.

His next move almost got him slapped.

"Are you crazy?" she shouted as he pulled the remnants of her tattered dress over her head, leaving her in only her bra, which hung lose and open.

"Nope, Austin, just sorry, real sorry." And he meant every word.

Even with the stinging ache still very real, she knew she'd forgive him. She loved him no matter how awful he was. How could she not forgive him?

She could have insisted he believe her before she ever agreed to make love with him, only for Hayden, it hadn't been making love.

It had been all out sex, nothing more. She would eventually learn to corral her emotions. To keep them pinned up deep inside where there was no chance they would escape and make her do really stupid things like believing that Hayden O'Malley loved her.

How fucking stupid can you get, Austin?

Well, she wouldn't be stupid any longer. From now on, she would do what was expected of her. Work, work and more work, and in between all that she would keep her nose clean, even if it meant staying home.

She shuddered at the thought but right now, what was most important was to make it through the rest of her six-month stint in O'Malley hell and get back in Judge Gumar's good graces.

Once accomplished, she would start venturing back out into the world.

Cool air caused her nipples to peak reminding her she was sitting on Hayden's bed, butt naked. Upon closer inspection, she realized he held a washcloth in his hand, a washbasin with steam rising from its surface sat on the bedside table.

When he started for her, she squeaked out, "What the hell do you plan to do with that?"

"Right my wrongs, at least the best I can for now so just lay back."

The man was a complete imbecile, she thought to herself.

"No way. Uh-uh, not even close," she muttered, trying to back further away from him only to be stopped by a hand on her ankle.

"Lie back, darlin'."

He spoke to her as if she was a few sandwiches short of a picnic, and it was starting to make her mad. Anger was a good thing. It would keep her from throwing herself at him begging him to take her, only slower this time.

Yes, she needed anger right now and embraced it like never before.

Kicking her foot at him, she twisted and tried to get away but it was no use. His hold was unrelenting, as firm as steel and in no way did he act as if he would let her loose anytime soon.

"Now, darlin'."

She struggled for a few more minutes just to be sure, before finally giving up. With a frustrated sigh, she lowered herself to the bed and tightly closed her eyes praying she wouldn't make a complete ass out of herself again.

"That's it, baby. Just relax and let me do all the work."

She couldn't imagine what work he was speaking of, could only guess what he had planned for the washcloth in his hand, and although she was sure her skin was beet red with embarrassment, she couldn't help the thrill of excitement rushing through her body.

"Oh." The sound escaped her lips before she could stop it as the warm washcloth covered her shaved mound. It made her tingle and helped her tight muscles to relax.

He gently caressed every single millimeter of her pussy with the terrycloth square, dipping it in the basin of steaming water between each swipe. She was in heaven.

It seemed like hours had passed when Hayden braced her thighs wider. Austin didn't mind if he would just keep up the blissful sensations. She didn't pay any attention when he shifted on the bed, leaving the warm cloth on her.

When the cloth was removed and replaced with something hotter and much more wicked, she jumped in surprise.

"Hayden?" she questioned, staring down at him, at his face buried deeply between her thighs.

"Mmmm," he hummed against her, the vibrations seemed to engulf her whole body. "Like honey, baby. Thick and sweet."

His words were naughty and sent a frisson of excitement spiraling throughout her body.

Her brain forgot what had happened earlier, allowing her body to take over. *Too bad my heart can't stay out of it*, Austin thought a minute before his tongue rasped over the swollen nub of her clit.

"Oh, oh, Hayden."

A single finger rimmed the soaked entrance of her vagina causing her to tense. When he didn't delve any deeper she relaxed again, thrusting her hands into his thick cap of russet-colored hair. It was silky beneath her fingers and felt erotic as it brushed her inner thighs.

The combination of sensations was enough to send her over the top. When tiny spasms tidal-waved through her body, Hayden murmured words of want, of encouragement.

"Come for me, baby, in my mouth, on my finger. Let me taste how sweet you are."

With his words came a new realization. His finger was buried deeply inside of her and there hadn't been a moment of discomfort.

Damn, he's good, she thought as her body tightened with the intensity of her orgasm, causing her to cry out in shock.

"Better than BOB any day," she mumbled before drifting off to sleep.

Hayden wasn't sure who or what "BOB" was and he wasn't sure he wanted to know. He was angry with himself for not having listened to Austin. And if he ever heard another of the town's residents talking down about her, there were going to be problems.

Austin stirred against him. Sexy little snuffling noises came from where her face was nestled into the pillow, bringing Hayden out of his thoughts. Pulling her into the curve of his body, Hayden snuggled the generous swell of her backside against his still-erect shaft. She may not realize it yet but she was now his, in every way. Hayden's last thoughts before drifting off to sleep were memories of Austin's sweet taste and breathy moans. Next time he would take things slow and show Austin just how good sex could be.

Chapter Eight

ℰℛ

She was really hard to get along with when she was in a snit, but she sure was pretty as hell that way. He couldn't help the chuckle that left his lips as she slammed the desk drawer for the tenth time, at least.

Evidently, she'd been in PMS hell all week, and was bound and determined to drag him with her. It was probably his fault to begin with seeing as how he'd refused to leave her alone since taking her virginity.

His chipper mood didn't last long as Austin continued to slam this and bang that. It was enough to give a man a headache. He could have easily gone outside to work but that would defeat the purpose of staying close to her.

Hayden didn't plan on leaving her sight during the day unless absolutely necessary. He stole as many kisses as possible and kept her body used to his touch. He figured that was the main reason why she stayed mad. Fighting her body's reaction to him was hard to do. He knew it and was using it against her.

He walked across the room and closed his hand over hers. If she slammed the cabinet door much more, it was going to fall off the hinges.

"That's enough for today, Hellion," he warned, feeling restless. Being close to her on a daily basis was hard but necessary if he planned to get her back in his bed.

Her eyes did their famous shooting daggers thing as they narrowed on him. "Let me go," she yelled, jumping to her feet.

She'd just started a running tirade on what an egotistical asshole he was when the phone rang. Hayden figured Austin wouldn't be finishing anytime soon so he waved her off and answered the phone himself.

"Yeah," he said as he picked up the line, only to hear nothing but silence on the other end. At least he thought it was silence but it was hard to tell over the volume of Austin's voice.

When there was still no answer he growled into the line, his patience all but gone, "Dammit! Is anybody there?"

"I'm here. What in the hell's wrong with you?" The familiar voice answered and demanded all in the same breath.

"Hey, baby brother." It was good to hear Zane's voice. It would be even better when they were all finally back together again.

"What in the hell is that, Hayden?" Zane asked when Austin's fit of temper reached an all-time high.

"Oh, hell, don't mind her none. It's just The Hellion," Hayden answered. "She got herself in trouble with Judge Gumar again so I've got her working here keeping my books."

"Austin?" Zane asked. Hayden could hear the laughter in this voice. "What did she do this time?"

"Her and that damned car, tearin' up the roads, sellin' her wares," he added in a disgusted voice. "Judge told her she could either get a real job or she could spend thirty days in jail. She opted for the job, and I needed a bookkeeper."

For some reason Zane thought the idea hilarious. His roaring laughter filled one ear as the sound of breaking glass filled the other. "Gotta go, baby brother. I think The Hellion needs a whoopin'."

He slammed the phone down. "Enough!" he roared in order to be heard above Austin's tirade.

Her eyes widened and her hands stilled, even her voice died down quickly. "I've had just about all the sass I can take from you. From now on, you'll act like an adult woman is supposed to act, and stop trying to run me off with your nasty temper."

When she remained silent, watching him intently, he moved slowly toward her. His eyes zeroed in on her heaving chest. She had worked herself up and her cheeks were all roses in the aftermath.

After holding himself back for more days than he cared to remember, Hayden felt as if he would explode. His cock stayed semi-rigid, his emotions in turmoil over the denial of his feelings.

He would admit to caring deeply for the woman standing in front of him but could he truly love her? He wasn't sure and didn't want to dwell on it. Not when there were so many more exciting things to think about and do.

"I'm going to kiss you, darlin'. This time it's going to be long, slow and deep. And when I'm done I'm going to take you over to the leather couch across the room there and make love to you the same way."

His words were sensual even to his own ears. They had a telling impact on Austin. Her body trembled. A shiver ran along her spine causing bumps to rise on her skin. And if he wasn't mistaken, the subtle scent of her arousal wafted gently through the air. Feminine and sweet, just the way she'd tasted.

His words sent a jolt of awareness straight to her core. His commanding presence made her want to struggle for freedom but she wouldn't.

She couldn't.

This time things would be different. She could see it in his eyes. In the tiny lines surrounding the hazel windows to his soul. He'd regretted taking her roughly, and it wouldn't happen again unless she explicitly asked for it.

She knew that much about Hayden O'Malley, and even if he didn't love her, for now it was enough.

When his arms engulfed her, she said nothing. The power of his kiss was all-consuming. It took her to new heights. The roughness was gone and although she knew she would at some point in time like to try a nice rough tumble, right now she wanted to be held close and loved slow. She needed it.

His tongue probed her lips until she parted them on a gasp. It was warm and moist, and insistent in its possession of her mouth. The way his hands bracketed her face made her feel cherished. The thumbs rubbing her cheeks were gentle as her head was titled back further for better access.

Breathing heavily, Hayden backed slightly away releasing the hold his mouth had on hers. Her lips felt tingly—the sensation seemed to arrow into a point at the apex of her thighs.

Her world tilted and whirled as Hayden firmly but gently lifted her with an arm at her knees and a hand at her back. Being cradled against the wide expanse of his rock-hard chest was an aphrodisiac unlike any other, causing her folds to slicken and gush. All of a sudden, she wanted nothing more than to have him buried deep inside her.

"Make love to me now, Hayden. Please."

After lowering her to the soft leather of the extra-wide sofa, he strode to the door and locked it. The click of the lock seemed to ring loudly throughout the room, taunting her with what was to come.

But she wouldn't be intimidated. This time they were both going to love every minute of everything they did. She wouldn't let it be otherwise.

Austin watched as Hayden slowly made his way across the room. His long-legged, loose-hipped stroll was all cowboy, sex personified. She hadn't thought she could get any wetter, but just watching him proved her wrong.

The pearl snaps of his shirt were all undone by the time he made it back to her. His bare chest was as inviting as a tall glass of cold water was to a man dying of thirst.

He was tanned a golden brown with a smattering of hair between his flat male nipples. Nipples her mouth watered to taste. The curly hair seemed to gather just before it narrowed and disappeared into the waist of his snug jeans.

The bulge beneath his fly seemed larger than last time, if that was possible, and for a fraction of a second she let the remembered pain he'd inadvertently caused scare her.

The look on her face must have told Hayden as much because without undressing further, he knelt before her until they were eye to eye and gathered her close.

"Don't worry, baby. It'll work out." His words were reassuring, the feel of his body against hers highly arousing.

She wanted him to know that this was something she wanted just as badly as he evidently did, but words seemed to stick in her throat so she decided to show him with action.

Splaying her hands across his chest, she pushed his unsnapped shirt off his shoulders. Leaning forward, she kissed first one nipple and then the other.

The sound of his sharply indrawn breath was like music to her ears. In what felt like minutes, they were both gloriously nude, a blanket draped across the leather surface of the couch beneath them.

When Hayden rolled over until she was sprawled across him, she gave him a questioning look. He seemed to understand completely what she was asking.

"This time you're in control, darlin'. I know it will all work, that your beautiful body can accommodate every inch of my cock, but I think for this time, at least, you'll feel better figuring that out for yourself."

Austin couldn't help the smile that crossed her lips. It was wicked in its intent and feminine with power.

"There is something I've always wanted to try—you got protection with you, cowboy?"

"Uh, yeah," he said not sounding at all sure. "In my wallet."

Austin retrieved the little foil packet then slid off of Hayden until she was on her knees on the floor.

"Turn around here so I can reach better."

He did as she asked without speaking a word although she could read the million questions flashing in the depths of his eyes. The twin orbs, normally hazel, were a deep moss green and beautiful beyond belief. She couldn't seem to pull her eyes away from his.

Taking a moment to gather her wandering thoughts, Austin racked her brain trying to remember the pictures she had seen, the articles she had read.

"Let me know if I do something wrong, okay?"

"Darlin', I'm not sure what you've got planned but in the position you are in, I doubt there could be a thing wrong with it."

She slowly opened the foil packet and when it was completely open, she removed the condom dropping the wrapper to the floor.

Reverently, as if unsure of how to proceed, she grasped the base of his jutting arousal with one hand. She couldn't help but wonder how he tasted, so before she placed the condom on him, she leaned forward and kissed the satiny-smooth surface.

Already dripping with pre-cum, his scent was mesmerizing. Feeling the dampness on her lips, she licked them then moaned in appreciation and surprise.

"You taste like…like, oh, I don't know how to explain it." She wasn't sure she would ever get enough of him now. It was as if a monster had been created.

"You're killing me, blue eyes." His hands were clenching the blanket tight. The white-knuckled fists proof that she was doing something right.

With her free hand, she placed the condom at the tip of his erect member and then ever so slowly she placed her mouth upon it, unrolling it as she engulfed him. His hips bucked sending a thrill through her body causing her pussy to gush.

When she was finished, she stood in front of him. "Can we do it this way, Hayden?" she asked.

"However you want, darlin'. Just remember I'm not used to being this patient. Don't tease me too much, or we might both end up regretting it."

"No teasin', Hayden. I promise. I'm so ready for you I might come before your cock even touches my pussy if we keep this up. I need you to fuck me now."

His groan filled the room. She wasn't sure if it was a groan of pleasure or one of disgust due to her language.

"Scoot forward for me." She felt the need to ride him and wanted to do it with him sitting so they could be close, as close as two bodies possibly could.

"Sure thing, darlin'," he said as he moved closer to the edge of the couch.

Austin climbed onto Hayden's lap, first one leg and then the other. Holding his shoulder with one hand, she guided him to her dripping center.

The flared head of his shaft stretched her until there should have been pain, but there was none. Instead, she felt full, consumed, as if she could live every day as she was now.

After a moment, she lowered herself until she was fully impaled. It felt wonderful and so right. Like there was no other place on the planet she belonged more.

It also scared her witless. She was in love, always had been and always would be, but in that instant, she realized the magnitude of what that meant.

Loving an O'Malley was hard enough. Loving an O'Malley who didn't love you back would be torture.

The feel of his thick and throbbing cock filling her left room for little thought. She cast aside leftover doubt, lifted her hips until he rested just inside her entrance then slowly lowered her hips until she felt his thighs beneath hers. It was mind-blowing to feel the enormity of her emotions as she rode him.

Chapter Nine

ဆာ

Her inner muscles gripped him so tightly he thought he would lose it instantly. Allowing Austin control over his body was not something he felt comfortable with.

Being in control was in his blood, in every inch of the flesh covering his body, but he wanted to make amends for his callousness. His rough treatment of her was inexcusable and yet she seemed to have forgiven him. The extent of her love, although she had never spoken the words, was truly amazing.

Grabbing her hips, he stopped her languid movement. "I know I said you were in control but if you don't hurry up, I'll be completely out of control," he gritted out.

Her eyes were bright, pupils dilated. A fine sheen of perspiration gathered on her upper lip. "And that's a bad thing?" Her voice was husky, the question taunting in its naughtiness.

"It is if I plan to keep my word, which I do. It'll be different next time though. I can promise you that much," he told her, squeezing her bottom tightly, causing her to squirm on his cock.

It drove him crazy to think she might like a bit of pain with her pleasure. That there was a possibility she would be up for a good paddling. He could feel his cock throb and grow even larger just thinking about it.

Leaning closer to her, he kissed her lips taking her full lower lip into his mouth and sucking. Drawing upon it as he planned to do with her erotically pierced nipples.

She moaned and pulled slightly away from him as if to break his hold upon her—he nipped her in response, she stilled instantly and moaned into his mouth.

Lifting her by the hips, he told her without words to continue or lose the control he'd given her.

Looking him straight in the eye, she slammed her body down upon his then gasped.

"Careful, baby."

Instead of words, she flung her head back, moaned loud and long and did it again. Before long, her pace increased and she was riding him as if there was no tomorrow.

The feelings she forced from his body were overpowering. He licked and kissed at her neck, drew deeply on her nipples as he played the twin silver bars with his tongue and teeth.

Her tempo increased until he could no longer think due to the intense pleasure he felt. Her inner muscles spasmed around him, alerting him she was getting close. He wanted nothing more than to make their first orgasm together an unforgettable one.

Reaching around her, he grasped hold of her bottom, gently spreading her cheeks. Her head flew up, her eyes open wide but he didn't stop, neither did she.

Wetting a single finger with her own juices, he then circled the tight bud of her anus until he zeroed in on the virgin bundle of nerves. She was shaking her head "no" but made no movement to stop.

Pressing slightly yet not entering her, he sent a whole new set of sensations coursing through her body. Her head stopped shaking side to side, instead resting in the crook of his shoulder as she came.

Her cry of completion filled the air. Her orgasm so intense he couldn't help but follow. Their shuddering bodies held and caressed each other until every last clenching muscle relaxed. Silent, replete, he sat there.

Still deeply embedded in her sated body, he wondered what it would be like to live the rest of his life with a woman like Austin Calhoun.

When he could find the strength, he lifted Austin from his lap. His semi-rigid length made him chuckle. It seemed there was no getting her out of his system. For once, he wasn't entirely sure that was what he wanted.

He wanted to love her but the past always seemed to flood back in, haunting him when he felt truly happy for the first time in years.

What if he fell the rest of the way and found himself in love? Would Austin then realize she had made a horrible mistake? If so, would she leave? The thought of it angered him.

It could very well happen. It had happened before when he was a young man, he didn't want to go through it again. Something warned him that if he gave in and Austin left him or used him in the same way his ex-fiancée had, he would lose more than just a diamond ring. That wasn't a chance he was willing to take.

The muscles in his body had stiffened, his mood now black, but he couldn't let her go. His arms tightened around her, protesting the mere thought of releasing her.

It was going to be a hard battle. How was it possible to hold Austin and not fall completely in love with her? And how, knowing her body inside and out as he did, could he ever let her go? He couldn't, and before all was said and done that alone would cause a firestorm of gigantic proportions.

Holding a woman without loving her wasn't right, but there was nothing on Earth that could persuade him to let her go. Austin belonged to him now and it would remain that way.

Arrogant and determined he may very well be but it wasn't something he was willing to change.

Warm and fuzzy feelings moved languidly about her body. Heaviness weighed her limbs down, too tired to fight it she didn't protest when Hayden moved as if to lift her from his lap.

In her mind, she thought he'd set her on the couch but she'd been wrong. Opening one eye a crack, she peeked up at his face. He was thinking and from the look of him, the thoughts weren't pleasant. His arms tightened almost painfully around her. She'd just opened her mouth to say something when his hold once again loosened and became the caressing hold she would dream of each night.

"Time to get dressed, Austin," he said. His voice a whisper against her ear, warm and reassuring when she knew damned well something was bothering him.

It was irritating to be kept in the dark and fed bullshit like a mushroom. She wanted to say as much but decided to hold off.

Instead she climbed from his lap, stretching lazily like a cat basking in the sun. Purposefully arching her back, thrusting her ass toward him.

"Ouch," she squeaked and jumped when he swatted the fleshy globe of her bottom. Heat spread, thrilling her. *It was amazing what a little love tap could accomplish*, she thought as her vagina flooded.

"That was just a warning not to tease me, Hellion. You deserve a whole lot more after your fit earlier," he said in a stern voice. "Next time I won't be so tolerant."

She had no idea what to think, but was extremely intrigued by the thought of being spanked. Idly she wondered if all it would take was another fit to test the waters.

Remembering the scowl he wore only moments ago, she decided to wait before trying his patience. Instead, she used her charms and taunted him with the possibility.

"Promises, promises," she purred, rubbing her large breasts against him as she passed. Once she retrieved her clothes from the hardwood floor of the office, she turned back to him.

His face was expressionless but his eyes told all. Heavy-lidded and sexy as all get out, they bespoke of how hard he was holding himself back.

He'd just removed the condom from his length, the purple tinge of his bulbous cock head teased her with possibility. He was once again hard and ready.

"You'd better believe it, blue eyes. Now get those clothes on and stop provoking me. If I whip that luscious ass of yours right now, I'll end up taking you again."

When she opened her mouth to speak, he held a hand up. "If I take you it'll be hard and fast and that wouldn't be good since you'll have trouble sitting as it is."

She wanted to argue but the tenderness between her thighs let her know he was right. When he came toward her, the scent of man and sex followed. She was so hungry for him she dropped to her knees without thinking.

"Darlin', you're trying my patience."

"Just a taste, Hayden. Then I'll get dressed, I promise."

Instead of telling her to go ahead, he clutched the back of her head with his large palm guiding her mouth to him. She licked him from base to tip sinking her tongue into the slitted hole. His hand tightened on her head, but he made no move to withdraw himself from her mouth.

She closed her lips tightly around his length working up and down like a woman out of control. Of its own accord, one of her hands roamed low, caressing his balls. The other hand held tightly to his hip.

Remembering how it had felt when he'd had his head buried between her thighs, she moaned low in her throat. She hoped the vibrations it sent along his flesh would be as exciting as it had been for her.

If the way his hips bucked against her face, forcing his cock to the back of her throat, was any indication then it had worked.

"Damn, darlin'. Don't stop." Funny, considering she wouldn't have been able to stop had her life depended on it.

Shaking her head slightly, without releasing him from her greedy mouth, she let him know that stopping was not an option.

Both of his hands were on her, rubbing her face, tickling her lips as they stretched to accommodate his cock. The feel of his work-roughened hands on her face as she sucked him off was arousing almost to the point of orgasm.

She wanted to finger herself but knew he wouldn't allow it. That thought made her hackles rise just a bit, but she obeyed the silent command. Later she'd give it some thought but for right now, she wanted nothing more than to taste him.

Leaving the tight sac of his testicles, she held his hips. Once again remembering the height of pleasure he had brought her, she decided to give it a shot.

Walking her fingers along his skin, across his narrow hips to the small to his back, she slowly ran one down the length of the crevice separating his ass. His hand stilled on her face, the one in her hair reached back and caught the wrist of the offending hand.

"I don't think so, baby," he chuckled.

She'd read that men could be funny about such things, but it had felt so overwhelmingly good when he had done it to her.

"But why?" she asked, backing off of his erect shaft enough to speak, then added, her cheeks hot. "You...uh... I mean...when you..."

"Yeah, blue eyes, I know, it felt good, and I'm glad because now that I've had you, I intend to have all of you."

Austin felt her eyes widen at the thought of his length and width, which was still bobbing in her face, fitting in that tiny hole.

Her eyes must have been bugging out of her head. "Don't worry. I'm not talking about now. That's something you've got to take slow, something we'll get to another day but it's not something we'll do to each other. Ever. So you might as well just forget it."

As he finished, his hand was leading her back to his engorged length.

"Spoilsport," she muttered just before descending upon him.

Working at a furious pace, she brought him to a knee-buckling orgasm. At least it would have been knee-buckling for her had she not already been on her knees.

Just the feel of his warm length in her mouth was enough to set her off. Combine that with all the excitingly frightening talk of anal sex and the taste of his seed, and she was lost.

She heard his shout of completion as she swallowed all he had to give but the rest was lost. The explosion taking place in her own body closed her mind to all but the insurmountable pleasure she was feeling.

With both hands at her cheeks, he leaned down and kissed her. He was slow in the exploration of her mouth, not at all turned off by the fact she'd just given him oral pleasures.

When he was finished and she was once again breathless, he stood then helped her from her kneeling position on the floor.

"Now, it's time to dress. No sass or you'll be sitting sore for a week and not only from a sore pussy."

It was funny how she had no trouble saying the words but hearing them come from Hayden made her blush every time.

Chapter Ten

✂

It was Friday night, time to visit Sean at O'Malley's. It never ceased to amaze him just how happy Sean looked these days. Hayden was happy for him. His brother was a big man with a big heart who deserved a classy lady like Honor at his side.

Tonight would be even better because Zane was back in town. Hayden felt relieved that the three of them would once again be together.

He thought over the conversation he'd had with his father just the week before. Sean and Zane would be just as happy as he'd been to speak with their father. Soon, they would once again resemble a happy family.

It took his eyes a minute to adjust to the lack of light. When he could see clearly, he scanned the tables and booths looking for Austin.

It irked him to automatically do so, but it was almost as if he was being internally pulled to possess her and if she was in the pub sitting on some pretty boy's lap there was definitely going to be problems.

"There's the old man now," he heard from the direction of the bar.

A thrill went through him at the voice. "Goddamned, baby brother. Look at how pretty you are." He couldn't help pulling Zane's chain. It was easy to tease him when every other soul in the place was dressed like your typical Texan except Zane who had on slacks and a collared shirt.

The woman next to him complemented his attire with her similar style of dress. Her beige slacks hugged an average frame, the scoop neck of her shirt showed just a hint of cleavage. It was the gold choker at her neck that gathered attention but the feature to hold his attention was the emerald green of her eyes.

"Serena," Zane spoke to her, his voice low, soothing. "Don't play him with your eyes, little one. He's a pro at the game."

Zane leaned in close to his woman, nipped her lower lip in what Hayden thought to be a bit of a rough love bite then in a whisper loud enough to be heard, he said, "He taught me all I know."

Hayden was intrigued by their relationship from that moment on. Serena gave a slight shiver at Zane's words and actions then lowered her lashes in what Hayden could have sworn to be a submissive manner before she held her hand out to him.

"Nice to meet you, Hayden. Zane has told me a lot about you and Sean, too," she said nodding to Sean where he stood behind the bar.

"You too, Serena. I'm glad you agreed to come home with Zane."

After embracing Zane in a bear hug, Hayden climbed up on the stool next to him. Needing to know but not wanting to ask outright, Hayden casually asked, "So, any excitement tonight?"

His ploy didn't work. Sean's eyes twinkled with mirth, his mouth split in a wide grin. "You mean has The Hellion been in? No not tonight, at least not yet."

Hayden knew he was being baited and decided to let the opportunity pass.

"Zane, did the two of you just get into town?" asked Hayden. "I would have waited out at the ranch had I known."

He watched his brother and Serena pass glances to each other. He could guess what the looks were about but decided to wait and see what they had to say. It didn't take long.

"We weren't really sure about staying at the ranch, Hayden. Didn't want to intrude. We have no idea how long it'll take us to find or build our own place."

Bingo! He'd guessed correctly. With the stern look of the oldest brother plastered on his face he said, "I'd like it if you stayed for a while at least." He meant every word. It would be nice having Zane around, and maybe Serena could keep Austin company and hopefully, out of trouble in the process.

Serena looked from Hayden then back to Zane. He nodded to her and gave a gentle squeeze where his hand rested on her upper thigh. Hayden thought it amazing how they communicated without saying a word.

"Thank you, Hayden. We'd love to stay with you."

"My pleasure, Serena. My pleasure." And it would be just to watch the two of them interact. Maybe he and The Hellion could take some lessons. That thought brought a smile to his lips.

About the time he was ready to leave, Honor came strolling by. Her smile was radiant as was the blush upon her cheeks. She looked like a woman who was thoroughly loved. Hayden remembered catching them in the throes of passion. The look on Honor's face as Sean brought her to orgasm standing right there behind the bar.

Never before had he considered himself a voyeur but watching them had excited him. Thinking about holding Austin that way brought his cock instantly to life. Maybe he'd just stop by her trailer and pay her a visit.

After talking to his brothers for a few more minutes, he passed the extra key he'd had made to Zane, said his goodbyes then excused himself. He was a man on a mission.

* * * * *

Fuck! I should have gone out tonight, Austin mumbled to herself. It was a Friday night, and she was sitting at home like some lovesick pup.

Her pussy throbbed with desire and she couldn't seem to keep her mind out of the gutter. It was absolutely amazing how often she thought of sex.

Damn, she swore as she felt the dampness of her panties against her bare nether lips. If she didn't get her mind off Hayden, she was going to go fucking nuts and probably run through every clean pair of panties she owned.

As she paced the tiny confines of her trailer, her thighs rubbed together sending her already intense arousal soaring even higher.

Just take care of it yourself, the little devil on her shoulder insisted.

She should call Hayden, but couldn't bring herself to do it. The thought of calling him up and begging for his cock was just too much. Talk about embarrassing, she'd die before that ever happened.

Sitting on her bed, she pulled a clear plastic box from beneath it. The contents were among her favorite. Different colors, shapes and sizes, almost every single one had at one time or another been lovingly used.

She'd just recently learned that no toy could replace a good man, but they sure did have their place. And their time, and right now just happened to be one of those times.

Removing the lid of her toy box, Austin picked out a red jelly vibrator. It could take a woman from a low moan to straight-out "Oh, My God!" in a matter of seconds. It was way up on the top of her list of favorites.

It took a minute to remove the short summer dress she'd been wearing but when she was done all that was left was a tiny red thong.

It matches my vibrator, she thought, cracking a smile.

Leaning back on her bed, she ran the vibe across her pelvis on its lowest setting while she played with her nipples.

Rubbing and rolling them felt wonderful. In ever-shrinking circular motions, she zeroed in on her already aroused clit. With the slightest bit of pressure, she ran the red tip of the vibrator over the swollen nub. The barrier of her panties and the light touch were just enough to tease.

When she could hold out no longer, she removed her panties and went to work. Her breasts were large enough that she could tease herself with her tongue. The moist warmth added to her excitement, the smooth surface of the vibrator made her insides protest.

When the need to be filled overtook her, she slipped the tapered vibe into her soaked cunt. The feel of it sliding in and out, lubricated with her own moisture was magnificent. The buzzing sound changed to a low pounding. *No, maybe it's my heart pounding in my chest,* she thought as she removed the vibe from her pussy. She couldn't help but wonder what it would feel like, so she ran it lightly over her anus then jumped at the contact.

She was getting too close. Gathering her vibrating egg in her other hand, she continued to tease the virgin spot between her ass cheeks with one toy while torturing her clit with the other. That was all it took to send her into orbit.

The pounding in her head grew louder as light shattered beneath her eyelids. Fresh air hit her face a fraction of a second before her hands were grasped, startling a gasp out of her, wrecking her perfect orgasm, making her extremely mad in the process.

"Dammit to hell, Hayden O'Malley. What in the fuck do you think you're doing?" she demanded as the slight tremors working their way through her inner thighs ceased.

"What am I doing?" he growled. "What in the hell do you think you're doing?"

Oh, the man was too much. If he thought she was going to be embarrassed and act coy, he had another think coming. This was her home he'd barged into and if he didn't want to see her masturbate then he could take a hike for all she cared.

"I was gettin' off, what the fuck did it look like I was doing?"

She watched as he took a deep breath then released it in a whoosh. He gathered himself, his anger lying just below the surface. She probably ought to be just a little bit afraid but she wasn't, she was mad. Mad as hell if the truth be told.

"I told you how I felt about that, darlin' —I swear to God, you don't listen for shit!"

"You weren't here so don't even give me that shit. You'd have never known if you hadn't come over. And just who in the hell are you to tell me when I can masturbate and when I can't?"

That seemed to do it. His eyes narrowed, his brows slashed together riding low over his eyes. He looked like an animal ready to pounce and Austin was ready for every minute of the pouncing she knew was coming, or at least she hoped she was.

"I'll tell you who I am and I'll tell you who you are so listen up real good, Hellion, 'cause I won't repeat myself."

His tone brought her temper to a boiling point. If he wasn't careful she was going to kick his cowboy ass right out of her trailer.

Austin climbed from the bed completely nude and completely unashamed by her lack of clothing. With a hand on her cocked hip, she lifted her chin to a dangerously stubborn angle then motioned for him to continue.

"I'm Hayden O'Malley and you're my woman. You'll do as I say and I say that unless I'm not available you'll come to me for your pleasure."

Austin couldn't help the incredulous laugh that burst from her mouth. What was funniest of all was the fact that he was absolutely serious.

Tears were rolling down her cheeks, her laughter still booming through the small confines of her trailer when he unceremoniously picked her up and tossed her on the bed.

"You want it so bad, Hellion, then go for it. You've got two minutes. If it doesn't happen in two minutes then you're mine. And believe me, once I've got my hands on you, it'll happen over and over and over."

The laughter died in her throat. His face was serious, his hazel eyes blazing a path right over her exposed breasts. "What in the hell are you talking about?"

"You, baby. You need to play with yourself so I'm giving you the opportunity, starting now," he said checking his watch.

"What in the fuck are you talking about?" she demanded.

"Play with yourself, Austin, in front of me, now. You've got," his eyes moved to his watch, "one minute and twenty-three seconds to come. Better get to work."

She wanted to argue, to protest but he didn't seem to be in the arguing mood. Besides, what in the hell did she have to lose? She was a master masturbator who knew just how to play her body.

Reaching for her red jelly vibe, she was brought up short when Hayden snatched it from her hand.

"Uh-uh, fingers only," he chided her, his eyes watching every move she made.

Holy hell! It wasn't nearly as easy as she'd thought it would be. Her normally brazen self felt extremely exposed, naked and open to his gaze the way she was. It wasn't going to work, and for the first time since he'd surprised her with his appearance, she wondered what was going to happen when she didn't orgasm in his time limit but due to her traitorous body, she'd soon find out.

Chapter Eleven

৯৩

He shouldn't have been so surprised but he was. The fact that she loved her toys was common knowledge. Hell, she rated the damned things and gave flyers out at her parties.

He just hadn't been prepared to see her fucking herself with a plastic cock when his worked perfectly well. It pissed him off that she hadn't tried to call.

When he'd pulled up in front of her trailer he was reminded of how inhospitable the box on wheels was. It was so tiny that a large man like him could feel mighty cramped inside. He'd never understood how she could live in such a small place.

He preferred wide-open spaces and would just as soon sleep under the stars as in the tin contraption she called home.

Hearing the sounds of her moaning as he'd stood outside her door had sent a chill up his spine. He'd just stood there for a minute trying to figure out what all the noise was about.

When she let loose a low and lusty moan he thought another man might be in there with her and instantly saw red. It was a good thing it had only been her vibrator.

The sight of her laying spread-eagle on the bed, completely naked had sent all the extra blood in his body surging just south of his belt buckle leaving his cock hard, heavy and ready.

"Time's up," he announced, taking in how her eyes had stayed focused on him.

He was angry enough to spit nails and didn't care if she saw it in his eyes or the rigid way he carried himself. Soon she'd be feeling it on her backside. The thought made his balls draw up close to his body, warning that he needed to get some control before he embarrassed himself.

"What in the hell has you so pissed? It's not like I was fucking another man, Hayden, and I won't give up my toys, so you might as well just go home and forget it."

She was trying to take his mind off of what she knew was coming. He'd warned her, and since she chose not to heed his warning, she could pay the price.

Clutching the thin red vibrator in his hand, he thrust it forward waving it in her face.

"This is what has me pissed off," he growled, then grabbed her hand and lowered it to the ever-present length of his aroused cock. The warmth of her hand over the thick denim sent his control on a downward spiral. The heat coursing through his body was unbearable.

"I seem to stay hot and hard for you, hellcat, through no power of my own. It's enough to frustrate the crap out of a man like me."

He watched her mouth open into a perfect little "O". Her lips plump and pink beckoned him but they would have to wait because if he kissed her right now, he'd lose it and they had some unfinished business to attend to.

"I may not be able to sit my horse tomorrow for fear of breaking this damned thing off," he snarled, pressing her hand tighter to the bulge beneath the fly of his jeans.

"Then I come over and find you screwing yourself with this tiny thing. I don't think so." He tossed the vibe onto the kitchen counter, flinging it from him as if it was the most offensive thing he'd ever seen.

The fit of his jeans was uncomfortably tight but for now, they would have to remain that way. He wouldn't chance her using his highly aroused state against him. If she pouted with that pretty bottom lip or brushed those magnificent breasts against him, he'd give in and she wouldn't get the spanking she deserved.

Setting her hand away from him, he stepped back and sat in the only chair he saw. It was a straight back chair with no arms, not very comfortable but perfect for what he had in mind.

"I warned you, darlin'. You knew just what would happen so you must want it as much as I want to give it to you."

His words made her cheeks flush. She was still sitting on the bed, her body gloriously nude for his view. Not once did she shy away or try to cover herself. Her confidence was one of the things that drew people to her.

"I don't know what in the hell you're talking about. You may have warned me but since I don't fucking belong to you, I didn't think your warning was worth a shit."

God but she was as ornery as they came. Her eyes sparkled and her breasts heaved. The rapid rise and fall of her chest as she filled her lungs with air set them in motion.

The pale globes bobbed and jiggled bringing his attention to the pink tips surrounded by darker, very large areolas. Much more than a handful "the gals" as he called them, always seemed ready for fun. The florescent lighting glinted off the silver bars, which ran right through the base of each erect berry.

His mouth watered in remembrance of their taste. Soon her ass would be a shade brighter than her beautiful nipples. His palm tingled in anticipation.

"You might not have heeded my warning this time, but I can almost guarantee you'll think about it the next time you decide to dig into your toy chest." He allowed his lips to curve wickedly. He couldn't wait to have her ass below his hand, the sound of flesh smacking flesh zinging through the tiny box on wheels.

"Now, come here. After I paddle that pretty, round ass of yours, I'll find something to keep those luscious lips busy," he said, his tone sensual yet no-nonsense as he leaned in for a kiss he hoped would curl her toes.

Surely the man had to be joking? Damn! He didn't look like he was joking. His eyes were shuttered, a muscle ticing in his square jaw.

His lip was slightly curved on one side giving him a rakish look. With his russet brown hair falling over his forehead, he looked just like the rogue on the cover of her latest bodice-ripping romance novel.

And he was going to spank her just like the hero in her book had spanked the heroine — just like she'd dreamed.

Try as she might, she couldn't keep from trembling at the thought. Her whole body shuddered in anticipation. Lifting herself from the bed, she walked the few paces it took to reach Hayden.

She'd just reached his side when he stood, towering over her for just a second before pulling her impossibly close. His kiss was hard and deep but didn't last very long. He pulled his lips from hers just before he sat, upending her over his lap in one swift motion.

"Oh," she gasped.

She wasn't given much time before he laid into her like a man possessed. The first blow to her ass was louder than it was painful, but surprised her into a high-pitched shriek just the same.

"Hush, darlin', or you'll have the neighbors runnin' to your rescue," he said as he raised his hand for the second time.

She bit her lip when the next one landed to keep from crying out. Her ass was on fire and she wasn't sure how much she would be able to take.

Just when she thought she'd no longer be able to keep quiet, he changed the momentum catching her off guard. No longer did his hand rain down as hard.

Now his large palm seemed to caress her burning flesh and every once in a while his fingers would dip between her thighs just enough to tease before he'd swat her again.

What in the hell is wrong with me that I like this? she wondered silently. The question didn't stay with her long when she felt him shift position. She was still draped precariously over his lap but something had diverted his attention.

"Grab the box, darlin'," he said, motioning to her toy box where it sat on the floor not far from his feet. When she hesitated, he grabbed and squeezed her stinging bottom sending a jolt of pleasure and pain right through her.

Snatching it up as quickly as she could, she struggled in her awkward position to hand it to him.

"Good girl," he said as he dug through it. What he was looking for, she had no idea.

"Hmmm, what have we here?" His tone was edged in steel causing a ripple of awareness to run up her spine. Husky and full of lust, the sound of his voice coursed over every exposed nerve on its way to her drenched pussy.

She heard a popping sound just before she felt cool liquid as it was drizzled between the cleft of her cheeks. She groaned in awareness, her body already taut with arousal. She wasn't at all sure how much more she could take.

When she tried to twist and turn on his lap to get a better view of which toy he'd decided to torture her with, he swatted her ass. "Stay put, Hellion."

She did as he commanded and with baited breath waited to see what his next move would be. It wasn't long before she felt his hands parting the cheeks of her bottom or the slight pressure of something against her.

"Have you ever used these beads, Austin?" he asked, his voice dripping with lust.

"N-no," she answered as he worked the first bead past the tight ring of muscle guarding her anal entrance. "I just got them, they're the only anal toy I own." She was extremely grateful she ordered the short strand in a small because if not she was sure she'd have exploded from the extreme sensations running through her body.

"Oh, oh, God!" she moaned as the second bead on the strand found its home within her.

The third and final bead made her burn as it was slowly pressed into her tight body. She was right on the edge of orgasm, all it would take was the slightest touch and she'd be there. That was her ultimate goal as she ground her hips against the hard length of his thighs.

"Not yet," he said swatting her bottom one last time as if for good measure. "Get up, blue eyes," he said helping her from his lap.

She felt full and her bottom burned where his hand had repeatedly landed. The look of his engorged cock behind the fly of his jeans was enough to make her mouth water.

She knew damned well what he had planned for her next. He'd warned her repeatedly to watch her cursing and she hadn't. She knew he meant business when he'd said he'd find something for her to do with her mouth. She couldn't help the smile that played at the corners of her full lips.

It wasn't exactly what she'd call punishment. There was just something extremely pleasing about being able to take the length of his cock deep into her mouth, to see and feel him shudder through his release. Today was no different.

Chapter Twelve

The sight of her kneeling before him knowing that she was filled with anal beads, wet and ready, made his heart pound and his cock throb. She was a woman unlike any other. The noises she'd made while he'd swatted her lush ass were erotic and made him think nasty thoughts, things, dirty things that would send them both into orgasm after shuddering orgasm.

At this point, there wasn't anything he wouldn't do for her, to her, except let her go hunting for the elusive walnut. The thought of that was enough to make his dick go limp. Now, the thought of tunneling his cock into her tight back passage was a whole different ballgame. He was sure when it finally happened, he'd come instantly because she was so tight.

She brought him out of his inner musings by lowering his jeans and boxer briefs, then wrapping her lips around the head of his cock and sucking hard. The sight of her hollowed cheeks as she drew on him sent his pulse to pounding. It felt as if his heart would pound its way right out of his chest.

The light scrape of Austin's teeth across the rigid underside of his shaft caused him to still due to the intense pleasure he felt. "Oh, yeah, baby. Just like that," he encouraged.

Her eyes peered up at him. As blue as the sky, he felt as if he were being carried away on a cloud. Tingling started low on his spine. His balls drew up against his body preparing to release his seed deep into her mouth. For some reason the thought didn't cause him to thrust further into her mouth.

Instead, he backed away, cool air replacing the moist warmth that had once engulfed him.

"I want to be deep inside of you when I come, darlin'," he said. It surprised him exactly how badly he needed to be buried deep inside her right now, this very second.

In just a few steps, they were back at her bed. He lowered her to the side of the bed, watching intently as she sat. Her eyes popped open when her full weight landed on the bed. He could imagine how the anal beads still clasped tightly within her body were pressed deeper as she sat.

When she started to scoot back, he climbed onto the bed. It was a very small bed, not really large enough for the two of them but they'd make do. When she had gone as far as she could, he mantled her body with his own.

Her legs opened wide for him allowing his hips to nestle into the spot her open legs created. He rubbed his erection against her opening then moved against her.

"When I push myself into your tight little pussy it'll be explosive. With those beads stretching you in back and me in front, you'll be filled beyond imagination." Just thinking of it sent a moist bead of pre-cum slipping from his cock. It was time to get out of his jeans.

Climbing back off the bed, he discarded every stitch of clothing he'd been wearing then climbed back up beside her. Lying on his side so there was enough room for the both of them, he played with her clit until she moaned and panted his name.

He continued with the torture of her swollen nub until she was grinding her pelvis against his hand. When her release was imminent, he gently pushed on the circular safety ring at the end of the strand of anal beads. Just a fraction of an inch he forced them further into her then pulled back on the ring until the first bead slowly crested the tight ring of her muscle but he didn't pull enough to allow her body to expel the bead.

The sensation must have overwhelmed her senses because her body tightened just before she crested, climaxing for what seemed like minutes. It was a beautiful sight to behold. Her face was flushed and misted with perspiration, her short hair was damp, making it look much darker than the shade of brown she had it dyed this week.

For the first time in years, he felt connected to a woman and that scared him. As much as he didn't want to admit it, it scared the hell out of him. Before he could pursue that line of thinking, she clasped her hands around his neck pulling him down close for a kiss.

Her mouth was like fuel for his weary soul. Her full breasts reminded him of melons ripe for the picking. Large and round their tips beckoned him to taste. With lips, teeth and tongue he paid homage to the puckered tip of each globe. When she was once again squirming beneath him, he quickly protected them, covered her body with his and thrust home.

"Oh, shit," she screamed as his cock tunneled into her tight slit. She was much tighter than normal thanks to the anal beads filling her rectum. He could feel them through the thin barrier of flesh surrounding them and wondered what it was like for her.

"You still with me, blue eyes?" he asked.

"Oh, God," she panted. "Hold on just a minute. I'm so…so full," she finally got out, holding his hips tight with both of her hands to still his movement.

He was afraid he might hurt her. He thought to pull out then decided to ask, "You okay, Austin? You need me to…" he started to say already pulling back when she grasped frantically at his hips. He could feel the tiny tremors coursing along her internal muscles. She was getting ready to climax and when she did, he wouldn't be far behind.

With the fist-tight hold her pussy had on his cock, he was lucky to have held out this long.

"Now, Hayden. Oh, God! Fuck me now, hard."

The sound of her voice filled the air around them as she pulled on his hips forcing him into her. It felt wonderful. She was tight and wet, writhing beneath him, her ankles clasped at his lower back.

He pounded into her, no longer worried about hurting her. The sounds coming from her were of pure pleasure. When her tight sheath clenched, milking him with deep, gripping spasms he gritted his teeth.

He wanted to hold out for just a moment longer. He still had one more trick up his sleeve and he planned to use it to send her into orbit one final time. Waiting for the right moment was extremely difficult considering his balls were about to explode.

When her body relaxed a bit and her tight pussy wasn't trying to strangle his cock, he reached a hand down and pressed firmly on her clit.

"I can't," she moaned. "Hayden, I—I can't," she protested when he changed to alternating between squeezing the tiny nub and firmly pressing on it.

"No choice, darlin'," he insisted. "Once more. Come for me now, Austin."

It was as if his words caused a chain reaction. He left her engorged clit and grasped the ring of the anal beads. Slowly he pulled all three beads free of her body. Her eyes widened as if in shock, her lips parted on a silent scream and her body convulsed in magnificent power as the beads stretched her one by one.

The sensation of the beads sliding from her body against the length of his cock, as it stayed buried deep within her pussy, sent him into an explosive orgasm.

* * * * *

Sun filtered through the tea towel that hung in place of a curtain in the tiny kitchen window. It was bright and cheery. Too bad she didn't feel the same way. She'd gotten up hours ago to use the restroom only to find herself deliciously sore and utterly alone. It was enough to mess up even the best of mornings. The fact she didn't have a diet soda in the place fucked it up all the more.

She was just about to dress and give the arrogant ass a call when her phone rang.

"Hello," she said not at all caring if she sounded friendly or not.

"Austin? Is that you?" the voice on the other line asked.

"Uh, yeah." She wasn't at all sure who'd called her.

"Oh, didn't sound like you. It's me, Honor."

"Hi, Honor, what's up?" Now that she recognized the voice, she was ready to talk.

"Well, we've sort of got a proposition for you."

"We?"

"Yeah, Serena and I. Have you met Serena yet?"

"Nope, sure haven't. She's Zane's fiancée, right?" she asked, genuinely interested in meeting the woman.

"Yeah, that's right," Honor said then continued. "Hey listen, we want you to get one of your parties together, tomorrow night if you can, at my place."

Austin pulled the receiver from her ear, looked at it as if it were something strange then put it back to her ear and said, "Are you sure about that, Honor? I don't think Sean's going to like the idea too much."

The other woman giggled into the phone, her voice giddy with excitement. "I know. That's the beauty of the whole thing. Zane and Sean have been so busy hanging out like they're high school chums instead of engaged men that Serena and I want to remind them we're here and hopefully have some fun in the process. Besides," Honor added, "I don't want Sean to think that just because we've decided to marry that I'm going to turn into some meek woman. Where would the fun in that be?"

"I gotcha," Austin announced, thinking this could be loads of fun if it was planned just right. "Leave it all to me."

Her mind was already whirling with ideas. It was exactly what she needed to keep her mind off Hayden.

"I'll see you both tomorrow night," she said then told Honor goodbye and hung up. Oh, yeah, tomorrow was going to be a hell of a night.

Austin spent the rest of the day making a list of the supplies she'd have to get from town, not to mention the inventory she'd have to pick up from the small storage unit she rented.

By late afternoon, she'd called a small group of women. The ones she knew wouldn't mind leaving early when the men showed up unannounced and uninvited and more than likely mad as hell if they were anything like Hayden.

He probably wouldn't make the effort but she would deal with it. After all, he'd probably be doing something very important at the ranch.

The man was among the last of a dying breed. A cowboy from the top of his hat to the toes of his boots and she loved him, but it really chapped her ass he couldn't get over the bitch who'd screwed him out of a diamond ring and his heart.

When she stole those from him, she'd also taken his ability to love. Knowing it was bad enough, admitting it was more painful than words could describe.

The night ahead was a long one rife with dreams. She was on her knees begging Hayden to stay with her.

Don't leave me, her dream self cried out to him.

She awoke with a start, sweating, her pajama top clinging to her breasts beneath. *There is no way in hell,* she vowed silently. *I'll never let it get that far.* It would hurt to watch him walk away when he decided it was time but she'd deal with it.

She had no choice unless she broke it off right now and for some reason, she just couldn't bring herself to do it. A tiny little spot in her held out hope that something deep inside of him would change. That he would wake up one morning and realize he loved her.

She snorted at the idiotic thought as she peeled herself out of bed and did her best to greet the morning.

"Dammit to hell," she mumbled while brushing her teeth, it was going to be a long day.

Most of it was spent trying not to think of Hayden. It wasn't easy and she wasn't doing a very good job of it but she hadn't expected to so it didn't really matter.

It took an hour before she decided on a color for her hair. She wanted something bright, something to help her regain her equilibrium. To help her be fearless, flippant and brassy as hell, just the way she'd always been.

Burgundy seemed like a good color so she went to work. The next forty-five minutes were spent with the smelliest dye imaginable on her head. It was so strong it made her eyes water.

Once styled, it was almost the color of eggplant, maybe just a bit redder but it would do.

She pulled on short denim skirt and a floral tank top. Added to it a pair of flip-flops and some dangly earrings and she was ready.

Everything was loaded lovingly into Jolene and Austin had just gone back into her trailer for her purse when there was a knock at the door.

She knew who was there before she even opened it. She was tempted to ignore him but knew he wouldn't go away and she had a party to attend, which gave her no choice but to deal with him.

Austin pushed the door open almost hitting him in the process. She kept her mouth closed. There was nothing friendly about her eyes and she knew it. It had taken years to learn how to shut others out. How to let their derogatory comments slide off her back. She was using all that learned knowledge to let Hayden know she wasn't happy with him.

Chapter Thirteen

ɷ

Hayden knew Austin wasn't happy the minute he set eyes on her. Hell, he'd seen blocks of ice warmer than she was right now.

Her thinly tweezed brows were narrowed at him, her eyes cold and hard making him feel like every kind of fool. He should have stayed or at least woken her up before he'd left but he hadn't.

He'd been overwhelmed by feelings he wasn't ready to deal with. Feelings he didn't know if he'd ever be ready to deal with. He cared a great deal about the woman standing before him, but he wouldn't be coerced into admitting to love he didn't feel.

He'd never understood why women insisted on hearing those three words. They might be simple for some but there was something about them that made his skin crawl.

It took a moment for him to notice she was all dressed up. Her hair was a different color. The deep dark purple made her skin look even paler, creamier. He wanted to lick her lips and see if she tasted the same. Instead of doing so or whispering sweet words in her ears, he opened his mouth and out popped, "Where do you think you're going dressed like that?" *Damn*, he swore under his breath. That wasn't going to get him anywhere with his stubborn hellcat.

"Not that it's any of your business but I've got a party tonight."

Her smile was smug. She knew exactly how much he hated the fact that she sold sex toys and how he worried about her going into strangers' homes and yet here she stood, proud as a peacock, rubbing it in.

107

"Damned if you are. The judge said you had to have a real job, Hellion, and you know it." His temper was getting away from him.

"I know exactly what the judge said, asshole, and I do have a real job. He didn't say a damned word about giving up my party-throwing." It was the truth so there wasn't much he could say in the way of a comeback.

He stepped forward feeling the need to hold her against him. To wrap her in his arms where he knew she'd be safe and sound, but was stopped short when she slammed the door in his face.

He heard the lock snick into place just before she yelled through the door.

"Go away. If you're not gone in two minutes I'm gonna call the police."

He wanted to rant and rave at her but it wouldn't do any good. He'd pissed her off right proper-like and until she had some time to cool down, they wouldn't be doing any talking.

He'd go visit Sean and have a couple of drinks before heading home. The damned stubborn woman was going to be the death of him.

Before leaving, he yelled through the tinfoil door, "At least tell me where your damned party is so I won't worry." It was disturbing how much time he spent worrying about her. He wouldn't let the why of that bog him down. It's just the way it was.

"I'll be fine. Serena and Honor will be there so don't worry about me."

Her words surprised the hell out of him and made him beyond angry. He wondered why Sean or Zane would agree to such a thing. He intended to find out.

Walking into O'Malley's always felt a bit like home. The friendly atmosphere and good company were a couple of the reasons why the place was so popular. The hulking man standing behind the bar was his main reason for visiting. His middle brother Sean had a heart of gold and a smile that could soothe the most frayed nerves. He also just happened to be one of the biggest people he knew. Sean O'Malley was one man you didn't want on your bad side.

Hayden stomped up to the bar and parked himself on the stool across from Sean.

"Beer?" Sean asked.

"Hell, no," Hayden replied. "Whiskey, make it a double."

"Problem?" Sean asked. Hayden could tell his brother was having trouble holding back his laughter.

"None of your damned business," Hayden growled, his black mood growing, as he downed his drink in one swallow.

"It can't be that bad," Sean said trying to lighten the mood. Hayden couldn't help but pierce him with an angry-eyed look.

"That damned woman is going to be the death of me. She's driving me crazy and I can't even fire her. How's that for stuck?" It was pitiful because Hayden knew beyond a shadow of a doubt that he wouldn't fire Austin even if she begged him to.

Sean asked what The Hellion had gotten herself into this time. The woman was always in some sort of trouble.

"She's doing another one of those damned parties tonight. I told her I didn't like her doing it, but do you think she'd listen?"

Hayden was in full swing, he couldn't seem to stop the tirade he'd started. "Hell, no! She told me I had no say in what she does. The thing that really chaps my ass is that she's right. Goddammit! I'd like to throttle the brat with my bare hands."

Sean seemed to be studying him in a way that Hayden didn't like. His eyes had taken on that faraway look and he'd gone tense all over.

"Did you say Austin's party was tonight?" Sean asked, his voice much too calm.

"As if you didn't know." Hayden still couldn't believe Sean would let Honor hang out with Austin. He could understand the benefit of a toy party, but Sean had made himself clear about Honor and Austin hanging out.

Now Sean seemed genuinely puzzled. "How in the hell would I know?" Sean demanded. "And when is the party because Austin was supposed to be getting together with Honor and Serena tonight? That's why she isn't here." Sean wiped his brow. "Oh, hell, no," he cursed, pulling the apron from around his hips.

"Where?" Sean demanded as he strode around the bar.

"How in the hell am I supposed to know? Austin slammed the door in my face before I could ask."

They were headed toward the door when it opened and in walked Zane. "Just in time, little brother."

"Where are you two going in such a hurry?" Zane asked, a puzzled look on his face.

"Us three, you mean. You're involved, too," Hayden answered.

Before Zane could say another word, Sean added, "Just come on. We'll tell you on the way."

Hayden had a sneaking suspicion Austin Calhoun wasn't going to be the only woman in trouble tonight. If the strained look on Sean's face and the wicked gleam in Zane's eyes were any indication, there were going to be some rosy red ass cheeks before the night was over.

* * * * *

Austin knew the three of them hadn't gotten away with a thing. It wouldn't be long before the three O'Malley men broke up their little party.

It had been fun so far. She'd done what she could to make sure the party flowed smoothly even though her nerves were so tight she thought she might snap. Talking openly with other women while hosting a party was always fun. Austin loved it when the guests at her parties had a good time.

Honor and Serena had interrogated her. It had taken everything she had in her to deny the feelings she felt for Hayden. They knew it, she could see it in their eyes and hated lying to them as well as herself, but it was the only thing she could think to do at the time to protect herself.

Austin was mentally preparing for the battle she was sure would come. Just thinking of Hayden brought her chin up a notch. She was in a stubborn mood and almost as excited about the upcoming confrontation, as she was nervous. It took every thing in her not to let her nervousness show. Instead, she told jokes and enjoyed the laughter of those around her.

Austin watched Serena and Honor closely. Honor seemed to flutter around the room as if the anticipation was too much. She seemed to be in awe of the large selection of toys Austin had set around the room, buying several for herself.

Serena, on the other hand, sat quietly. Her fingers rubbed over the gold choker she always wore. They trembled slightly with each pass over the gold's gleaming surface making Austin speculate whether or not they might have carried the ruse a bit too far. As she continued to watch Serena, Austin noticed the way her eyes almost glowed with excitement. Her head was cocked to the side as if she were listening, waiting.

There wasn't even a knock before the door flew open. It banged into the wall behind it. The sound was loud as it reverberated throughout the room.

She'd been ready for hours. Wrapping her stubborn pride around her like a shield, she'd prepared for just this moment.

Winking at Honor, she mouthed the words, "Let the games begin."

Three very large, very imposing men stood on the threshold of the door. She couldn't focus on anyone but

Hayden. The room cleared, women excusing themselves one by one then leaving.

Tension was mounting. It was so thick you could scoop it with a spoon. Everything seemed to happen in a blur of activity.

Completely fascinated, Austin watched as Sean lifted Honor to her feet. A warm smile crossed her lips before she made a comment to him about being home early. Austin didn't believe for a minute that, that particular comment would get Honor very far where Sean was concerned.

Austin figured she'd have to play it up just a bit. The whole thing had been planned to help her new friends after all. "Son of a bitch, Sean. Ya couldn't wait 'til the party was over? Those women you just scared off seemed real interested in ordering some of my stuff." She motioned around the room bringing attention to the assortment of toys.

The look on Sean's face as he followed her gestures, finally noticing the assortment of dildos and vibrators, was priceless. When his hand slowly wandered the length of Honor's back before settling on her ass, Austin mentally patted herself on the back.

One down, one to go.

Austin shifted her attention to where Zane stood holding Serena in front of him. Those two needed no help, was Austin's first and final thought as Zane lowered his head to speak to Serena. A look of pure contentment crossed her face before she turned and strode from the room.

Zane's hazel eyes pinned her to the spot. "You can collect for this later," he said, lifting a red leather flogger from the coffee table.

The thought of leather against her ass was beyond her comprehension. Would she like that as much as she'd liked the palm of Hayden's hand against her ass?

Sean said something to Hayden about taking care of her while he took care of Honor and it royally pissed her off.

She began collecting her stuff, thrusting them into the empty duffle in disarray instead of neatly packing as usual.

"I don't need you to take care of me, Hayden O'Malley." She tried to hide the hurt in her voice but it was no use.

"It's after hours, I'll do as I damned well please. I'm beginning to think that thirty days with Judge Gumar might just be safer anyway."

She needed to get away from him. She'd been in love with him since just after her ninth birthday and never once did she think a day would come that she'd be willing to give up that love but it had.

It just hurt too damned much to love and not be loved back. She'd go see the judge and do what he asked—it was the only way she would get out of the mess she'd created with at least a tiny bit of her heart intact.

Chapter Fourteen

ဢ

Hayden tried not to think about the hurt in Austin's voice. He wanted to take her home and drop her off so he could think. He needed some time alone to figure out what the next step was.

When he reached for the duffle she'd just stuffed full of sex toys of all different shapes and sizes, she batted his hand away.

"Don't you touch any of my stuff, you big ass. You gave up that right when you climbed out of my bed without so much as a word."

That sounded too much like a kiss-off for Hayden's liking.

"The hell I did," he snarled, his voice low and ominous. He wasn't ready to give her up completely, he just wasn't ready for a commitment. Couldn't the damned woman understand that?

She might if you ever took the time to tell her that you at least care, the voice in his head taunted.

He'd do that, just as soon as he had some time to think it over, they'd talk. Until then, she belonged to him and he'd touch every inch of her body if he damned well pleased.

Hayden led Austin from the house. "Now get in and stop arguing."

"I've got my own car, Hayden. I'm not leaving Jolene here."

The wind had kicked up and it looked like it might storm. One never could tell what would come out of a little Texas wind.

"Yes, Austin. Tonight you are. I'm giving you a lift home if I have to pick you up and put you in the cab. Make up your mind. It looks like rain's comin'."

It was a lame excuse but he was willing to use just about anything. Continuing to stare her down, he was glad to see when she shrugged as if it made no difference then climbed into his truck.

The ride back to her trailer was silent and not the friendly type of silence between two companions. This silence yawned around him like a deep chasm making his shoulders tight with tension.

He was glad when he finally reached her door. After he placed her duffle inside, he turned to her and took her into his arms.

The kiss was hot and hard. He was angry at the both of them but hadn't meant to punish her in such a way.

"Fuck, Hayden. I wish to hell you'd stop doing that." The fact she didn't want his kiss irked him. He wanted to hold her so tight against him that she'd feel every inch of his engorged cock and she didn't even want a damned kiss.

"And I wish you'd watch that filthy mouth. Why can't you be more like Honor? Now that's one classy lady."

He regretted the words the minute they were out. Her face paled and her eyes pooled with unshed tears but it didn't last long. In the next instant, she was on him like flies on shit.

"If you don't like who I am then you can go straight to hell, Hayden O'Malley, because believe me when I say that you're not the catch of a lifetime either."

Each word was punctuated with a finger to the chest forcing him to step back, taking him closer to the door.

"We've all got our faults and if mine are too much for you then it's probably a good thing I never told you exactly how much I love you."

It seemed like his heart stopped beating. He'd known she loved him. Every time she looked at him, he could see it in the deep pools of her blue eyes but he'd never heard her say the words.

She seemed just as surprised as he felt. Her face had gone even paler if that was possible. Her demeanor worried him.

"Just go already. I've made a big enough ass out of myself for one day, Hayden. Don't you think?"

Her shoulders slumped in defeat. Turning on her heel, she disappeared into the tiny, closet-sized bathroom and locked the door behind her.

He wasn't at all sure what he was going to do now. His heart urged him to break down the door and pull her out of there. She made his life complicated as hell but for the first time in years, he felt complete.

On the other hand, he remembered exactly what it had felt like to be the fool. To give his heart to a woman who wanted him only for his money and the status being a rancher's wife would bring her. He needed some time to think.

As he pulled back onto the highway, he had an odd feeling that he shouldn't wait to talk to Austin but he ignored it. Tomorrow would be soon enough.

Only it wasn't tomorrow when he was jerked from a restless sleep by somebody pounding on his front door.

"Hold on," he grouched as he fumbled with a pair of jeans.

The pounding didn't slow. If anything, it became louder.

"I said hold on just a damned minute." No more grumbling. He was wide awake now as he bellowed down the hall.

When he'd finally managed to wrestle his jeans on, he stomped from the room to see who in the hell would dare come to the Big O in the middle of the night.

He was ready to lay into someone but changed his mind when he swung the heavy wooden door open and found his father there. Soaked to the bone and covered with mud, his father had a frantic look on his face.

"What is it?" Hayden insisted. "What's happened?" He looked past his father but saw no one else.

"You've got to come into town son. You're needed."

"All right, just calm down and tell me what's going on," he said as he strode into the house.

Turning on the light, he made his way to the room for his boots, grabbing a shirt along the way.

"A tornado touched down in town," he heard his father say. His ears started to ring and he almost let panic set in before gaining control over his emotions.

"Zane and Sean?" he asked. Zane and Serena had decided to stay in town at a motel after the party break-up. They'd left a message on his answering machine letting him know.

"They're fine son, Sean and Honor, too. The only place damaged was the trailer park."

He was on his way out the door before his father could get another word out. He wouldn't be able to get there fast enough and his hands were shaking so badly he wasn't at all sure he'd make it in one piece.

He didn't want to ask but he had to know. "Austin?"

"There have been no reported deaths, numerous injuries but no deaths so far. The only thing is, Austin's trailer is a complete loss and she is as of yet unaccounted for. I was hoping she was here on the ranch with you but…"

* * * * *

It took a moment for the darkness to recede but even then, everything seemed blurry. All around her it was quiet. After the freight train-like noise, the silence was eerie.

There were voices but they sounded so far away and she couldn't seem to get her bearings so she had no idea which way to go to find them.

Something had happened but for the life of her, she couldn't remember what it was. All she knew was that she needed help and she needed to get out of wherever it was she was lying.

Bracing her hands on the ground…the ground? Why was she outside? Damn, something wasn't right.

Austin tried to push herself up, but there was something heavy on top of her. After a few minutes, she gave up and tried to kick out with her leg only to feel excruciating pain shoot all the way to her thigh. Oh, shit! Something definitely wasn't right.

Using her hands, she banged loudly against whatever was on top of her and yelled. Her voice was hoarse at first and came out as more of a croak but soon she was up to her full lung potential and was squalling like a wild banshee.

When she thought she'd lose her voice she quieted down. Taking a break from the efforts to remove herself, she listened intently. The voices were getting closer. Her heart pounded in her chest at the thought of them overlooking where she was trapped.

"Help me!" she sobbed. Her voice seemed to echo back at her causing her head to hurt even more. She couldn't let the pain stop her so she pounded and yelled. "Somebody help me."

When the voices drew closer until she could make out someone calling her name, she yelled, "Over here! I'm over here."

The shifting of whatever was on top of her made her leg hurt so bad she felt lightheaded. With everything she had, with everything she was, she held on. She had to be sure they wouldn't miss her.

The weight on top of her shifted again and she thought they'd kill her trying to rescue her.

"Oh, God, stop. Please stop." Complaining was not her intention but the blinding pain in her leg left her no choice in the matter. And then she heard his voice.

"Austin! Austin can you hear me?"

"I can hear you. Hayden, please don't let them move it anymore, it hurts." The tears rolling down her face tasted salty but reminded her she was alive and was going to make it out of this. His next words gave her no alternative.

"Hold on, baby, just hold on." She couldn't help but cry out at the pain. "I love you, darlin'. Do you hear me, Austin? Don't you leave me, okay?"

She had no more time to talk. It seemed as if everything around her erupted in chaos. She was told they would have her out in a minute then warned that the heavy object on top of her was going to be moved.

The pain as it was done left her breathless but she held on. She had to know for sure that Hayden was really there and that he really loved her. When she was free of the heavy weight, his was the first face she saw.

He wiped the tears from her cheeks and leaned in to kiss her very lightly on her lips. His eyes shone bright but he wouldn't pick her up and hold her—she couldn't understand why.

"Stay still, the paramedics are on their way." Now she understood his reluctance to move her.

"Tell me," she insisted her voice barely a whisper.

"I love you. I don't deserve you, but I love you with all I am."

They were the words she had waited so long to hear. They seemed to set her free and hold her tight all at the same time.

They were the last words she heard before the blackness overtook her.

Chapter Fifteen

80

Hayden still couldn't believe how lucky she had been and how lucky he was. A slight concussion and a badly broken leg had been the extent of her injuries when she was ripped from her trailer and blindsided by a huge billboard.

The stubborn woman didn't make a very good patient. Hayden secretly believed the doctor who treated her at the hospital was happy to see her go considering she had cussed him out more than once in her drug-induced stupor.

The past two weeks had been hard on the both of them but it accomplished two very important things. He'd been forced to come to terms with his true feelings for the obnoxious woman he loved, body, heart and soul and she'd had no choice but to move in with him.

Zane and Serena had found a house in town they loved and had spent the past few days moving. But by far, the most exciting thing was the fact that he'd gotten down on bended knee and proposed. Austin had been so happy she'd clobbered him with her bulky cast while trying to throw herself in his arms. He still had the bruise to prove it.

"Hayden," she called from the kitchen interrupting his thoughts. It was something she was good at, something that would take some getting used to.

"Yeah, darlin'," he answered as he made his way to her, her cast-covered foot resting on a pillow on a chair across from her.

"Are you sure your dad doesn't mind giving all three of us away? I know he seemed happy when I asked him but Serena and Honor did ask first."

"Austin, if you don't want to have a triple wedding just say so. I'll go with whatever you want. I just want it to be real soon." He waggled his brows suggestively. Her cast had put a damper on their sex life but not much. It continued to amaze him how well they fit together, in every way possible.

"No, I want to. I already feel close with your dad. I just don't want to intrude."

"You're not. We're not, so let's just do it, okay?"

"Okay," she answered then moaned when he kissed her lips passionately. "I can't wait until I'm your wife, Mr. O'Malley."

He nibbled her ear as his hand caressed the taut tip of her breast. "Neither can I my little Texas tornado."

* * * * *

It was an improvement, she thought wryly. To go from Hellion to Texas tornado would have to do because it seemed like all she was going to get for now.

When he licked her ear then whispered seductively in it, she felt her pussy spasm, soaking her panties.

"When you are Mrs. O'Malley I'll have you every night and every day and when you're a naughty girl, I'll paddle your ass just the way you like."

"Thanks for the warning, Hayden," she chuckled. "Now let's go. We've got a rehearsal to attend if we plan on getting married with the rest of the crew."

She smiled when he groaned as if not having her right then and there was going to kill him.

"You big ole baby," she taunted him as she struggled to the door on her crutches.

The wedding rehearsal went off without a hitch. Austin enjoyed every minute of her time afterward visiting with her soon-to-be new family. Her mind was spinning with excitement at the knowledge that Hayden loved her. Becoming Mrs. Hayden O'Malley would be a dream come true.

Later that night, Austin cursed her crutches as she struggled into one of Hayden's threadbare T-shirts. It barely reached the top of her thighs thanks to her large breasts. The thin cotton fabric showed more than it covered but it didn't matter. If she knew Hayden at all, she wouldn't be wearing it for very long.

By the time she finished, Austin was ready to throw the crutches across the room. The dull ache in her leg reminded her just how stupid that outburst would be.

"You all right in there?" Hayden called from the bedroom.

Austin opened the bathroom door, banging it against her crutch, almost tripping in the process. She swore a blue streak before finally looking up. Hayden was sitting on the bed in nothing but his boxer briefs, making tsking noises at her.

"Don't even go there," she groused. "These damned things are going to drive me nuts." She said the last as she clumsily made her way across the room. When she reached the bed, Hayden grasped her waist, holding her steady.

"Here, darlin', let me take those," he said, pulling the crutches from her grasp. His large, warm hand still at her waist coaxed her onto the bed before leaning the crutches against the wall.

Austin watched as Hayden moved up her body very slowly being extra careful of her fractured leg. He stopped when his mouth was even with her breasts. His warm breath feathered over one puckered nipple, wringing a low sensual moan from her lips.

"I'm going to take you slow and sweet tonight, Austin, just like you deserve."

Hayden's voice was smooth, flowing over her body, sensitizing nerve endings that were begging for attention. Through the thin cotton of the shirt she wore, Hayden latched onto a peaked nipple. Teasing and torturing it, he laved and sucked until the moist heat of his mouth dampened the shirt.

Releasing her cloth-covered flesh, Hayden backed up the tiniest bit and stared. The heat of his gaze over her nearly exposed flesh made Austin crazy with need.

"Hayden," Austin gasped, trying to pull his head back to her.

"No, baby. Slow and sweet, remember?"

Austin thought she would go insane if he didn't do something. A single finger traced first one breast and then the other in ever decreasing circles but he never touched her nipples. Austin was getting ready to make her needs known when Hayden's hand started traveling lower on her body.

When he stopped, spreading his fingers wide on her lower abdomen, she wanted to scream. When his mouth followed, blazing a trail down her belly to her pussy, she knew she would scream. His touch was like magic and torture all rolled into one.

His tongue flicked the swollen nub of Austin's clit causing her hips to buck. "Oh, Hayden," she moaned, grasping his hair in her hands.

Hayden chuckled before backing off to look at her. "Put your hands over your head, darlin'." Austin heard his words and even understood them but couldn't bring herself to comply. With every beat of her heart, she wanted to urge him back to his spot between her legs.

"My way or no way, Austin, and this time it's going to be slow and sweet." He lowered his head until the heat of his breath tortured her clit. "Put them above your head, baby."

His thumbs spread her labia, baring her clit even more so that every breath feathered across the sensitized bundle of nerves. Austin would have walked over hot coals at that moment to get him to lick her, to taste her.

"Good girl," he murmured against her when she did as he asked, raising her arms above her head.

Austin was sure she would die when Hayden's tongue swiped the length of her slit, his hands now holding her thighs wide. The feel of his mouth on her was so intense she couldn't hold back the shuddering orgasm that washed over her like a tidal wave.

Before her mind stopped swimming, Hayden was on her, in her. Buried balls-deep inside of her, Hayden stopped all movements, taking the time to kiss Austin as if there would be no tomorrow.

She could taste herself on his lips as he nibbled and sucked her bottom lip just before he languidly stroked her tongue with his.

Austin lifted her good leg, resting her heel on his flank in hopes of driving his cock deeper inside of her, all the while cursing her cumbersome cast. "Please, Hayden."

"Anything for you, darlin'," he said then started a rhythm of long slow strokes that lifted her higher and higher until her body could handle no more. Austin's inner muscles gripped his length as she climaxed. Hayden wasn't far behind.

His body stiffened above her, a groan of sheer pleasure filled the room as Hayden's cock swelled further before finally spilling deep inside her. Hayden turned to the side taking her with him. Sated, Austin snuggled into the curve of Hayden's body. "I love you," she said sleepily.

"I love you too, darlin'," Hayden answered, pulling her body closer to his. When the darkness of sleep descended, Austin dreamed of her wedding night.

TYING THE KNOT

෨

Dedication

Aunt Barb, thank you for your strength and support throughout the years. I love you!

Trademarks Acknowledgement

The author acknowledges the trademarked status and trademark owners of the following wordmarks mentioned in this work of fiction:

Black Hills Gold: Black Hills Jewelry Manufacturing Company Corporation

Stetson: John B. Stetson, Company Corporation

Velcro: Velcro Industries B.V. Ltd Liab Co

Chapter One

ಬ

It was good to have his boys back together, Collin O'Malley thought as he fought to tie his tie. It had been a while since they had all been together as a family. For the most part, it was his fault his sons had stayed away. He never should have hounded them about following in his footsteps. *Better late than never*, he thought to himself.

Adding three daughters to the equation was more than he ever could have hoped for. The fact they had asked him to walk them down the aisle was like icing on the cake.

"Now if I can only get this blasted tie right," he muttered into the quiet room.

A suit and tie were bad enough, but a tuxedo was pure torture. Collin lowered his hands from his lapel and wondered for the umpteenth time what in the hell made him think he could tie a bow tie.

"Should have bought a clip-on one you old fool," he scolded himself looking at his reflection in the mirror.

His brown hair was now gray at the temples but Collin didn't worry about such things. He might be past his prime but he was no slouch, his broad shoulders and steady gaze were proof enough of that.

After fiddling with his tie for a few more minutes, Collin admitted defeat. Frustrated beyond belief, he took a deep breath and just stood there staring into the mirror.

He'd never been overly fond of ranch life, which was why he'd become a lawyer instead of a rancher but the room he saw behind him told a story all its own. The well-worn comforter — a family heirloom — was beautifully displayed on the antique bed.

The room was cozy and comfortable and except for the pristine white paint on the walls, a person might think they'd taken a step back in time. Everything was just the way Hayden preferred it. Simple. Collin felt deep pride in the life and home his oldest son had made for himself.

Collin's chest puffed up with pride just thinking about the ceremony to come, but first he had to figure out how to tie his tie.

Now I'm going to have to go find someone to do it for me and there is no telling what I'll come upon. Collin chuckled, turning from the mirror. Since arriving at the Big O Ranch, he'd had to shoo his sons away several times. He'd actually caught his youngest son Zane red-handed.

He had been trying to sneak into the room where his soon-to-be wife Serena was dressing. It had been so much fun to sneak up behind him.

"And just what do you think you're doing?"

Collin tried to keep his voice stern, which stopped Zane dead in his tracks. One hand still on the knob another holding a large jeweler's box.

He was the epitome of the traditional groom. His black tux was meticulously tailored, his shoes polished to a high shine. Only the scowl marring his facial features didn't match that of a groom on his wedding day.

"Thought I'd give Serena her wedding gift now," Zane said as he'd turned to face his father, giving away no indication of the havoc he'd planned once he'd snuck into the room like a thief in the night.

It amazed Collin just how much Zane resembled him in his younger days. Wavy brown hair fell over his forehead. The hazel eyes staring back at him could be his own. Eye color was the one thing that seemed to have passed from generation to generation of O'Malley men.

"Now, Zane, you know the ladies don't want to be seen before they're walking down the aisle. Here," Collin said reaching a hand out for the box, "I'll give it to her for you."

The change in Zane was immediate. His body stiffened and his eyes became feral, which Collin thought hilarious since he was the father and not a rival.

"She gets this only from me. By my hand."

Collin had seen the gold choker collar Serena never went without. He might be old but he also knew what it meant. It showed possession and Serena wore it proudly, something not commonly seen in this new day and age. Collin decided not to push although it would be a whole passel of fun to do so.

"Have it your way, son, but save it for after the wedding."

Zane just stood there for a minute before giving a curt nod of his head and heading down the hall. Collin couldn't help the booming laughter that followed causing Serena's door to open a crack.

"Did he leave?"

"Yes, dear, he's gone."

She opened the door a bit more but not enough to allow entrance and took a quick peek down the hall. "That man is being a nuisance," she huffed, a hand perched on the swell of her robed hip.

"It probably had something to do with that pact you three cooked up," Collin said referring to the fact all three women had decided two days ago they needed some time to prepare. Once the decision had been made, they had packed enough clothes for a few days and then gone into town to rent a motel room leaving only a short note in their wake. To say his boys had been angry at the time or on edge since, would be putting it mildly.

Shaking himself from his thoughts, Collin started toward the door. Maybe he'd be lucky enough to find one of his other sons pacing the study like a caged animal. The chances one of them would know how to tie a bow tie was slim to none but it was worth a try.

Before he could make it to the door there was a knock. And before he had time to even open his mouth to bid the visitor entrance, the door was flung open. Collin's eyes almost popped out of his head when Austin, better known as The Hellion by those who knew her and fiancée to his oldest son Hayden, came hobbling into the room.

Her gown was definitely eye-catching. Collin wondered if Hayden had seen it yet. The skirt of the gown fell around her feet like a pool of shimmering cream but it was the top part that garnered attention. What appeared to be a corset hugged her body closely drawing her waist in leaving no place else for the generous swell of her chest to go but up. Her hair was once again a soft blonde, making her pixie-like face look innocent. The woman had a penchant for dying her hair the most outrageous colors. It was one of her quirks, along with driving too fast, cussing too much and selling adult sex toys, which gave his old-fashioned cowboy of a son fits.

"What's wrong?" Collin asked genuinely worried.

"Nothing except that this damned thing is almost as uncomfortable as the crutches."

Austin lifted the hem of her dress until Collin could see the blue of the Velcro shoe the doctor had given her to use over her cast. It took the place of the crutches, but evidently, it proved to be just as bothersome.

"Why did I have to be the one thrown around by a tornado and break my leg? And your son won't leave me alone. What is it with you O'Malley men anyway?"

She continued to rant and rave as she hobbled closer. Collin didn't argue with her. He couldn't have gotten a word in edgewise had he tried.

"And don't you give me that look, Dad, I've seen you eyeballing poor Mrs. Granger like you could just gobble her up."

Collin choked on a strangled laugh at the same time warmth invaded his heart. He absolutely loved to hear the girls call him "Dad" but he didn't figure he needed to share the fact he had been doing exactly as accused. He also didn't see the need to explain that Ethel Granger didn't seem to mind one bit. So he kept his mouth closed.

Austin finally made it across the room. Between the length of her dress and the cast shoe, it wasn't an easy task. She fiddled with his tie as she talked. She was like a freight train headed for a derailment, she was wound so tight. Collin just stood there and listened, praying the whole time that she didn't strangle him with his own tie.

Collin had known Austin for as long as he could remember. She'd grown up locally raising hell, earning her nickname The Hellion. Vibrant and headstrong, she was one fine match for Hayden.

"And I told him I didn't need a honeymoon. I don't *want* a honeymoon. Why in the hell doesn't he listen? Is it so hard to understand that I like being on the ranch?"

She went on and on until Collin was sure his tie was going to be in shreds. His legs were also getting ready to give out from the way he'd been standing with his knees bent in order to allow for Austin's lack of height.

"He'll come around," Collin said, grasping Austin's hands in his. He gave them a little shake to catch her attention. "Do you know of anyone who might be able to tie one of these?"

Austin looked up at his face then back to his throat, her face turned red. "Good Lord! Why didn't you say something?"

Collin wanted to laugh. He could only imagine what his still untied tie looked like after being mauled by a nervous Austin.

"I bet Honor knows how," she finally said then proceeded to tow him out the door as quickly as her cast-covered leg would allow. Once in the hall she turned to him. "I'm going to go check on Serena since it's getting close to show time."

Collin nodded his head then made his way to the room he knew Honor was using to get ready. He was reaching to knock on the door when he heard the first shriek.

"Sean O'Malley, you'd better get out of here."

Collin knocked loudly. It was more of a bang than a knock. He figured that ought to put a stop to whatever was happening.

"Come in."

"Go away."

Both orders were given simultaneously so Collin decided to ignore the booming masculine voice of his middle son Sean and heed Honor's bid to enter. He opened the door then quickly spun around.

The tiny glimpse he did get was of a partially dressed Honor backed against the armoire, held in place by his burly son. The man was built like a wall with arms. His smooth-shaven head made him look menacing, which helped when nights at his business O'Malley's Pub became rowdy.

"Sean, there's no time for this. Now get downstairs and pace with your brothers."

There was an exasperated sign behind him then some low-spoken words. Sean soon stalked past him with a scowl on his face. Collin just smiled and said over his shoulder, "Holler when you're decent, Honor," as the largest of his sons continued down the hall.

It was only a minute before Honor was back at the door. Her hair was done up in some type of sophisticated twist and held in place by pearled clips, she looked absolutely stunning.

"That man," she said wagging her finger, "is a menace."

Collin agreed, however, didn't think it was the right time to tell her that by leaving the couple days before, the three of them had opened themselves up for all sorts of strange behavior from the loves of their lives. He figured they'd find out firsthand tonight. So once again, he kept quiet.

"Oh, here, let me do that," she said stepping forward reaching for his tie. Collin prayed his tie wouldn't get mauled again. It was only seconds though before he was pleasantly surprised by a beautiful smile and a pat on his chest.

"There you go."

He was given no time to say a word before she shooed him out of the room exclaiming she was going to be late for her own wedding if she didn't get her dress on. He made his way down the hall and eventually into the study where he found his sons. It wasn't much later that they were all notified it was time to take their places.

A beaming Collin had a word with each son before sending him out the front door and into the yard where the wedding was to take place. He watched as his sons fought to remain outwardly calm knowing full well how they felt inside. He'd felt the same way all those years ago when he'd married their mother.

Before his thoughts had chance to take hold, Collin caught sight of his soon-to-be daughters-in-law. They were all dazzling in their own way.

Serena's gown fell from thin straps to a scoop in the front showing just a hint of what was beneath, giving her a classy look. It was when she turned around that Collin damn near swallowed his tongue.

What there was of a back, fell to the uppermost swell of her backside in the same scoop fashion as the front. The champagne color gave her fair skin a rosy glow.

Turning his attention to Honor, Collin wasn't at all surprised to find her wearing a traditional white dress. The high neckline and straight skirt did nothing to take away from her beauty. If anything she looked regal, elegant.

It amazed Collin how different the three of them were, and yet, how close they had become. He smiled broadly anticipating the look on his sons' faces when they finally got to see their brides.

Once on the freshly painted veranda-style porch, Serena and Austin each took an arm. Honor stood on the other side of Austin, helping with her dress so she didn't end up sprawled indignantly across the white runner leading to the altar.

It was a beautifully sunny day with the birds singing merrily. The grassy expanse of the Big O Ranch's large yard was crowded with guests, the perfect setting for an outdoor wedding. And except for the wicked twinkle in three sets of hazel eyes, one might have mistakenly thought the O'Malley brothers were behaving themselves for once.

Collin knew better, of course. He didn't figure they would last very long at their own wedding reception. He couldn't help but smile as he escorted the nervous brides up the aisle to their impatient grooms.

Chapter Two

ဢ

Zane tugged Serena up the long corridor. Her small hand clasped tightly within his much larger, impatient hand. He couldn't wait to touch and taste her, to tease and torture every curve of her body.

Even as hungry as he was for her, Zane couldn't help but chuckle at the way he and his brothers had chosen to leave their own wedding reception.

The band had been playing, the dance floor packed with guests. The setting sun and mild breeze kept everyone cool as they enjoyed the outdoor reception at the Big O Ranch.

After the first dance on the slightly elevated wooden dance floor covering a large portion of the ranch yard where the wedding ceremony itself had taken place, the O'Malley boys had been forced to stand aside and watch as their wives were passed from well-wisher to well-wisher.

Zane couldn't have kept his eyes off Rena to save his life. After holding her close for that first dance, his body expected nothing less than for him to carry her off and make passionate love to her.

Serena had taken being tossed over his shoulder with nothing more than irritation and stiffness for being pulled off the dance floor and away from the revelry early.

Austin on the other hand had left cursing soundly, something only the flat of Hayden's hand on her backside would be able to deal with. And Honor had been somewhere on the complete opposite end of the spectrum. The last Zane had seen of her and Sean, Honor had all but undressed him from her upside down vantage point, her hands running over the flesh of Sean's back beneath the un-tucked waist of his shirt.

Zane cleared his mind of all but he and Serena as he led her down the long hall toward the bridal suite he'd reserved for the night.

Serena's rapid breaths were like music to his ears. Her husky whisper caused his control to slip another notch. "Hurry, Zane. I need you inside me so bad."

Zane stopped dead in his tracks causing Serena to run into him. With quick, efficient movements, he backed her against the wall.

"I want you completely naked, Rena, by my hand. When we get to the room, I'll undress you so slowly you'll be begging me to take you before I'm done."

After saying the words, Zane took Serena's mouth in a kiss so sizzling hot he couldn't help but grind his rock-hard cock against her. The brief, heated taste of her lips was enough to quench his thirst for the moment, enough to allow him to drag her back to the room. He had an interesting and fulfilling night planned for his new bride.

Zane wasted no time getting to their room, quickly closing the door behind them. Serena kept her eyes trained on him, never once straying to the opulent surroundings of the room. For a moment he thought to ask her what she thought of the place and all he'd done to make it special for her—for them. Looking deeply into her eyes once again, Zane decided against it. There would be time enough later.

"Do you have any idea how beautiful you look?" Her dazzling green eyes were locked on his. "I couldn't have waited another minute to have you to myself."

Zane watched Serena's eyes widen at his words. Her cheeks flushed then her eyes lowered. Heavy-lidded and aroused, they told a story without the benefit of words.

"Come to me," Zane commanded, holding his arms open until she flowed into his hold.

Breathing deeply of her womanly scent, Zane lifted his hands to her shoulders and, with deft fingers, began lowering the tiny straps holding her dress in place.

It was slow going and took every ounce of Zane's willpower not to rip the dress from her body. To appease his need to touch, to taste, Zane lowered his head possessing Serena's mouth with a need they both knew well.

She tasted sweet, her lips soft and warm. She lightly flicked her tongue across his lower lip just the way he liked. The way she knew would drive him insane with need.

Zane took possession of the kiss, deepening the strokes of his tongue in her mouth. When Serena's body melted against his, Zane left her mouth. His lips sought the curve of her jaw then moved with slow, languorous movements to the lobe of her ear where he nipped and sucked until she was writhing against him, tiny mewling sounds coming from her parted lips.

When the silky fabric caught on her nipples, Zane groaned then stripped it from her body allowing it to fall around her feet like a shimmering pool of champagne. Her barely there thong panties and lace-top hose held up by garters set his senses reeling, making it virtually impossible to keep in control. Serena stood before him, completely nude except for her garters, hose, thongs and shoes. He liked the look and decided to keep her that way for now.

Zane's mouth watered to taste but there was still something he wanted to do to make the night unforgettable. He could tell his words affected Serena because her breasts swayed enticingly with every quickened breath she took. "But first I have something I want to give you."

Zane left Serena for a moment to retrieve the gift he'd tried to give her before the wedding. Holding the large jeweler's box in one hand, he opened it with the other, watching her face carefully as he did so.

As soon as the box was completely opened, Serena's eyes snapped to his. Shimmering with unshed tears, she fingered the gold choker she wore faithfully.

"It's beautiful," she finally choked out, no longer able to hold back the emotions coursing through her body.

"It'll be even more beautiful on you, baby."

Zane closed in on his new bride. With deft fingers he unclasped her intricate gold choker and replaced it with the new one he'd had commissioned as her wedding gift.

The design was much the same with the main difference being in the multi-hued Black Hills gold. It looked stunning against her pale skin. Zane hadn't realized he'd said the words aloud until Serena answered him.

"Thank you. God, Zane, I need you!" The words were a mere whisper against his lips as she arched against him aligning her heat with the hardness of his arousal.

"You've truly been mine for several months now, Rena, but today things have changed. Today, adding this ring to your finger..." he started, stroking the band of gold on the ring finger of her left hand. "It made me so much more aware of who you are. Who I am and who we'll become together."

Serena kissed him again, deepening their passion until Zane had no grasp of time or reality, only of the woman in his arms and the fierce love he felt every time he held her, possessed her.

"I'll never let you go, I love you too much to even consider it."

Her lower lip trembled as she opened her mouth to speak but no words came out.

"Mine," Zane growled.

"Yours," she finally got out. "Forever yours."

Fishing in the pocket of his slacks, Zane pulled free a generous length of black silk. He lifted the piece of silk so Serena could see it. Her cheeks flushed and her nipples pebbled. Zane was sure if he traced a finger across the folds of her pussy, she'd be wet and ready and so hot she would burn him alive.

"Turn around," Zane said, his voice low and husky as he slid the blindfold over her surprised eyes. "I want you to concentrate on feeling everything I do to you, with you."

"Please, Zane." The tip of her pink tongue darted out to moisten her lips causing his shaft to throb in readiness.

"Around, baby."

She did as he asked. When he'd tied the length of silk snugly behind her head, completely covering her eyes, Zane lifted her into his arms, cradling her close to his chest as he made his way to the bedroom. He walked across the room and sat Serena down on a chair situated in the corner of the room.

She sat just as he'd placed her. Her only movement was to cock her head to the side as he began to remove his clothes. Serena shivered when he moved closer to her, slowly lowering his zipper. He could feel her warmth. It was as if it came off of her in waves searching only for him.

When Serena blindly reached for him, Zane grasped both of her hands in his. "Later you will be bound to my bed by the softest silk but for now you will only be bound by my words."

"No, Zane, I want to touch you," she pouted. Her full lower lip protruded a bit, enticing him beyond belief.

Zane wondered if Serena could hear him over the panting breaths, which seemed forced from her lungs. Leaning in close, he nipped her lower lip not bothering to sooth the small bite of pain with his tongue. His next words made her squirm in her seat.

"You belong to me, Rena. This might be our wedding night but some things will never change. Disobey me and you'll be punished. Do you understand?" Zane purposefully kept his words low with an edge to them.

A sexy smile widened her lips as she answered, "Yes." Zane couldn't help but wonder if she'd push merely for the spanking that would result.

"Good girl. Now put your hands behind your back and keep them there until I tell you otherwise."

When Serena did as she was told, Zane stepped closer gathering her face in his hands. The feel of her warm skin against his palms was familiar. The sensation of her warm breath as she parted her lips to allow the head of his shaft entrance was like heaven.

"So hot, Rena. Do you have any idea how hot it is to watch my cock disappear between your pretty pink lips?"

Serena groaned in the back of her throat at his words. She loved it when he talked dirty to her and he knew it. She pulled off his still-hard shaft then, grasping it firmly at the base, she licked in one long stroke to the tip paying extra-special attention to the very sensitive underside of his head.

Zane was lost so deeply in the exquisite feelings her mouth on him were provoking that he never even considered punishing her for using her hands when he'd instructed her to keep them behind her back.

"Is it as good as when I watch you sink into me?"

Zane sucked in a breath at Serena's provocative words. "I don't think anything is as hot as watching me between your thighs except maybe to see your body struggle to accept me from behind as inch by inch of my cock disappears into your tight ass."

Her breath hissed out, vibrating along his shaft causing a tingling sensation to start at the base. Zane's balls drew up close to his body warning he was getting close.

"Beautiful," he said as she swirled her tongue around and around. His fingers caressed her cheek, tracing her widely parted lips as they sucked and tasted him. One particularly strong stroke brought him closer. The light graze of her teeth against his sensitive cock head brought him to completion. His shout of release as he came in Serena's mouth vibrated off the walls.

Back to his senses, Zane was surprised to find he was still standing. His knees felt weak, his legs like jelly, and yet, his cock was still semi-erect. He was sure he'd never get enough of Serena O'Malley.

* * * * *

The room smelled faintly of roses. Not overpoweringly so, just enough to tease and tantalize her senses. Not being able to see was always hard to get used to but the reward was worth the sacrifice. It hadn't even occurred to her to look around. All she could think of was Zane and the fact she was now Mrs. O'Malley. Nothing else seemed as important.

Her body hummed with need. The taste of Zane alone was almost enough to make her come. Wound tight, Serena feared she might fire out of control if he didn't do something soon.

"Zane."

A brief second later he was at her side. "Tell me, baby."

Serena hesitated. Not because she didn't know what to say or what she wanted but because her senses were so overloaded she couldn't seem to put two words together much less a complete sentence.

"Now, Rena," he said, tweaking the hard peak of her nipple. The slight pain his action produced seemed to center her, yet it made her burn even hotter than before.

"Make love to me, Zane. Please."

Zane helped her to her feet with a hand at her elbow then slowly led her closer to the bed where he removed her blindfold. It took Serena's eyes a moment to adjust but when they did, she couldn't help but stare.

The room was huge. The bed she was sitting on took the whole center. Its four posters were draped with some frothy fabric giving it a very romantic feel but it wasn't the room itself that had her mouth gaping open like a fish out of water, it was the fresh rose petals strewn about.

With her shoes still on, Serena hadn't felt them as she'd been led into the room but they appeared to be scattered everywhere and in all different colors. She turned to Zane who was watching her, a loving smile curving his lips.

"It's beautiful."

He kissed her tenderly then knelt before her removing first one shoe and then the other. "I know how much you love roses," he said keeping his gaze locked on hers.

Smiling back, Serena fingered the new gold choker adorning her neck. "And Black Hills gold."

Zane inclined his head then gathered a few petals in his hand before moving closer to her. His eyes never left hers. Passionate, intense, they drew her to him. Zane lifted a blood red petal between his fingers then traced it around her lips. Soft and silky, the scent tantalized her already heightened senses.

Soon the crushed petal was dropped to the floor, a light kiss replaced it when he lowered his lips to hers. Afterward, Serena wrapped her arms around Zane, hugging him close, her cheek pressed tightly against the broad expanse of his chest. Serena couldn't help but inhale deeply, loving his manly scent.

Zane loosened her arms from around his waist then held her at arm's length. "On the bed, baby."

Serena scrambled to do his bidding, hoping that soon he would touch her in all the places her body longed to be touched. Sitting in the center of the bed, Serena watched as Zane climbed up beside her. His body moved with grace. The muscles of his arms and chest bunched with his every move.

Zane pulled out several lengths of the same black silk he'd used to blindfold her. Serena couldn't help the excitement that coursed through her system as a result. She loved to be dominated by Zane, to give him pleasure and take all he had to offer.

"Hands above your head, baby."

Serena remained quiet but did as Zane asked. Lying on her back, she stretched her arms above her head and waited with baited breath while he bound them together, positioning her body the way he wanted then securing her arms to one corner of the bed.

"Now, Zane." She felt on edge, so very close and yet so far.

"Shhh," he crooned as his hands roamed her body, warm yet firm.

His fingers circled her nipples, never quite touching them. Serena couldn't help but arch her back as she squirmed to get closer to his touch.

"Touch me." Her voice sounded husky even to her own ears.

The next thing she knew, his mouth covered one of her turgid nipples. Teeth nipping, tongue lapping, Zane brought her to the brink then backed away.

"Like that, baby?"

"Oh, yes. More."

Zane lowered himself down to her, causing Serena to tense. He trailed her body with hands and lips until he was resting between her parted thighs. His breath was warm as it feathered across her mound.

The first flick of his tongue sent her senses into overdrive. It wouldn't take long before she was seeing stars, she thought as he buried his face against her heated center. Her internal muscles spasmed with need then clenched tightly around his finger as he steadily pressed into her.

"Are you ready?"

She could hardly think much less speak. Her body was moving all on its own, her hips thrusting in time with the movement of the finger he was tormenting her with.

"Yes," she gasped as his mouth once again found her clit, sucking hard.

"Then come for me."

His commanding words sent her flying. The feel of his tongue stroking her intimately kept her there. Over and over, wave after insurmountable wave racked her body leaving her panting for air, her body limp and sated.

Serena felt as though she was floating on a cloud. Her head was spinning with the strength of her orgasm and yet she was still ready, still hungry for more. Zane tugged her hands free of the bed then released them from the length of silk he'd taken great pleasure in using to bind her.

She kept her eyes closed the entire time he worked to free her, the entire time he rubbed her wrists, caressed her arms and shoulders. When he lay next to her, gathering her close, Serena couldn't help but wonder what was next. She lifted her head with plans to ask what was on her mind but Zane beat her to the punch.

"Tonight is your night, Rena. To do with me as you please."

Serena stared at him wide-eyed. It had never occurred to her to want to take the upper hand in their sexual relationship. She enjoyed being possessed by Zane but there was a bit of curiosity growing within her at his words. The fact he was willing to give up control was mind-boggling. To think he loved her enough to allow her free reign of his body, of what would happen between them over the next several hours made tears come to her eyes.

"Are you sure?" she asked sniffling back tears.

"I'm yours, baby."

Serena decided it was too good an offer to pass up so she did the first thing that came to mind. The one thing she was sure would drive him absolutely crazy—she tied him to the bed just as he had done to her on numerous occasions.

Not quite sure of what to do first to tease and erotically torture her bound captive, Serena decided to experiment. She trailed her mouth across his chest and lower, nipping and laving his flesh while he groaned and cursed.

She came close but never quite touched all the places she knew would bring him to the precipice then push him over, wondering the whole time if he felt as out of control as she always seemed to feel when he had her in the same situation.

When he was panting for breath, his hands still securely held out of the way, Serena straddled his hips then lowered herself slowly until she was completely impaled upon his shaft.

Serena noticed Zane's tightly closed eyes and the fine sheen of sweat covering his body. His hands were curled into fists around the ties that bound him.

Leaning forward, Serena placed her palms against Zane's chest and was met by the thundering of his heart.

Zane's breath hitched. "Damn. Fuck. So good, so tight…" His words trailed off with her languid, deliberate movements, furrows of concentration appeared between his brows.

"Watch me," she whispered, raising her hands to her breasts when he opened his eyes.

Playing with her nipples, Serena proceeded to make Zane curse, groan and sweat, and she enjoyed every minute of it.

"Faster, Rena," Zane commanded, thrusting his hips up until he'd lifted her almost completely off the mattress.

The movement caused his shaft to delve impossibly deeper, making Serena cry out. Her body was on fire and each time he sank home, it only became worse.

"Oh, my God," she panted, leaning into Zane for a kiss. She sucked his lip, ate at his mouth like a woman possessed.

Breaking the kiss, Serena used a hand on his chest to lever herself back up. Once there, she fingered the sensitive bud of her clit while rocking against Zane in search of release. No longer able to hold back, she quickened her pace.

"Oh, shit… Oh…" was all she managed to gasp as her body bowed. The nonstop spasms that rocked her internal muscles took her breath away.

Zane's deep growl warned of his imminent release. His cock swelled within her slick passage, every exposed nerve ending tingled with his movement. The warmth of his essence filling her sent Serena over the edge and into oblivion once again.

Once again breathing normally, Serena untied Zane then snuggled against him. With her cheek to his chest, she could hear the rapid beat of his heart. She placed her hand over it, loving the feel of the steady staccato beneath her palm.

"Done torturing me already?" His words ended on a breathless chuckle.

Serena's body tingled in places she didn't remember existed. Her upper legs still trembled and twitched from riding Zane to completion. Her mind was working in slow motion, ready for sleep.

"Um-hmm," she muttered. "Too much work."

Zane kissed her temple lightly. "I love you," he whispered. Those were the last words Serena remembered before drifting off to sleep in the arms of her husband.

Chapter Three

ഉ

"Knock that off," Sean scolded as he strode from the reception with Honor over his shoulder.

She was doing everything possible to strip him bare in record time. The feel of her hands on the flesh of his back brought his cock raging to life. The surge of arousal Sean felt was instantaneous. He could literally feel the blood pulsing through his veins with every touch from Honor's hands.

"Dammit, Honor!"

Her only answer was a muffled giggle before the warmth of her tongue met the flesh of his back where her fingers had just tortured. Sean couldn't help the groan that escaped his lips. The rough sound that welled from deep within him must have made her even hornier because the next thing Sean knew, Honor had a hand down the waistband of his slacks, cupping his ass.

Another giggle echoed from behind him. "Mmm, buns of steel," she said, squeezing his cheek. Sean chuckled at Honor's antics yet wondered what in the hell had gotten into her.

"Honor?"

"Sean," she said then giggled yet again.

"You been drinkin', Little Darlin'?"

"Just punch."

Sean chuckled, lowering Honor to her feet when they reached his truck. "Up you go," he said helping her in through the open driver's side door. He could only imagine what had been added to the punch. Sean figured it was a good thing he'd carried Honor off before she ended up more than just tipsy.

Seated behind the wheel, Sean held Honor close with a hand on her thigh. Instead of tugging away as she once would have, Honor snuggled closer to him. Her slender body was plastered along his side, her warmth radiated right through his clothes making him long to strip them both down to their skin. The light floral scent of her perfume drifted lightly making him long to feel the warmth of her bare skin against his.

She had the softest skin and so very sensitive. She marked very easy, something Sean went through great pains to make sure didn't happen, but sometimes they just got way too involved in their lovemaking. Not only was her skin soft but she tasted so sweet on his tongue. The thought of her finding her release against his mouth made his cock ache. Remembering the sultry noises she made as she bucked against his mouth made it virtually impossible to concentrate on the road.

"When we get to the room, I'm going to taste every inch of you, Little Darlin'."

Honor gave him a saucy smile. Her eyes were glazed with lust, her cheeks flushed. His fingers rested a breath away from her moist center over the silky white fabric of her wedding gown and Sean made sure she knew it. He stroked and teased, loving the way the muscles of her thighs bunched. He was so involved in what he was doing and her reaction he barely heard her words.

"That's the neat thing about being the passenger," she said. "I don't have to wait until we get to the room to taste you."

The words had no more left her mouth than she scooted her hips away from him and leaned into his lap. Sean sucked in a breath as Honor struggled to loosen his belt and unfasten his slacks.

Sean fumbled beside him looking for the button that would move the seat back. Cool night air engulfed his engorged length the minute she released his cock from the confines of his pants and underwear, but it did nothing to lessen the magnitude of his arousal. Especially when her moist tongue peeked out, flicking across the sensitive head of his shaft.

"Oh, hell," he groaned, grabbing a handful of Honor's blonde hair, wrapping its length around his fist to bring her closer. The strands of her hair felt soft against his hand. Sean used his hold on her hair to anchor her to his lap, to guide her, knowing she loved every minute of it.

The breath whooshed from his chest when Honor took him to the back of her throat. She hummed her approval then proceeded to lick and nibble her way back up his shaft.

"Damn, baby." Sean's words wheezed from his chest.

"You like that?"

Her face was a mask of concentration as she looked up into his face. Her blue eyes wicked, intent as they studied his face. Her eyes trained on his. Even as Honor watched him, her hand continued to stroke the length of his shaft, keeping him teetering on the edge.

"More than you'll ever know," Sean hissed between clenched teeth.

He pulled his gaze away from hers when the lights from an oncoming vehicle caught his attention. "Damn, Little Darlin', you're going to get us killed." Honor merely smiled and winked before she once again lowered her head, taking him completely within the warm confines of her mouth.

Sean could feel the muscles of Honor's throat as she worked him like a pro. Being in her mouth was warm and hot, almost as good as being buried hilt-deep inside her tight little pussy.

"Oh, yeah. Just like that, darlin', just like that."

The whole situation was frustrating as hell. He had to keep at least one hand on the wheel and his eyes on the road. Either that or pull over, and that option wasn't on the agenda since in Sean's mind, there was nothing more important than getting Honor to their honeymoon suite so he could fuck the living daylights out of her.

Sean wanted nothing more than to pull off his pants, spread his thighs wide and let Honor truly get down to business. One touch of her fingers on his balls and he'd be shooting off like a rocket.

Instead, his inebriated new wife was maniacally torturing him to death. Wife? He liked the sound of that. Damn, life was good, Sean thought as his hips bucked seemingly of their own accord.

"You're getting close," she said, pulling back. The heat of her breath wafted over his cock making him shudder, his need was so strong. "Come in my mouth, Sean."

Honor lowered her head and sucked him deep, leaving him no choice but to do what she asked. The tightening of Sean's leg muscles caused him to accelerate briefly before he regained his senses. As much as he didn't want to, it seemed he had no choice in the matter. It was either pull over or get them killed, so Sean pulled his truck to the side of the road.

With his forehead on the steering wheel, he sucked in several lungfuls of air. He'd just turned toward Honor who had the widest smile splitting her face when a set of red flashing lights pulled up behind them.

"Son of a bitch," Sean muttered as he straightened his clothes.

Honor giggled, the sound filling the cab of the truck. "Tell him we're just taking a blowjob break." Sean rolled his eyes and prayed that the half-drunk minx sitting beside him would keep quiet.

"Hey, Sean. Everything all right?" the officer asked when Sean rolled down his window.

Why did it have to be a local sheriff? Why couldn't it have been one of the highway patrol officers who frequented the area but didn't live locally? "Oh, hell, I'll never live this down," he mumbled under his breath. To the officer, Sean gave a roguish smile and winked. "Yeah, everything's okay."

The officer nodded his head, smiled at Sean then winked at Honor before he turned and ambled off toward his car. Sean waited several minutes after the patrol car drove away before inching his truck back onto the road. His heart was still trying to pound its way out of his chest and his legs felt as weak as a newborn foal's. It was a good thing he didn't have to walk to the motel.

Honor scooted close to him again. This time, instead of driving him crazy with her mouth, she teased and tortured him with her wandering fingers.

Sean grasped her wrist gently yet firmly, stopping the circles she was drawing high on his inner thigh. "That's enough, Little Darlin'," he growled.

"Not nearly enough," she growled back.

Honor's mock growl was anything but fierce. Her wide-eyed innocent stare combined with the way she'd scrunched her nose up to attempt the growl made Sean laugh. Hell, she was so damned cute all drunk and horny, something Sean had only glimpsed before. That time though had been one of sorrow and pain, nothing like the woman sitting beside him now.

"Your ass is mine when we get to the room, Honor O'Malley. You've caused enough trouble for one night."

"Promises, promises," she giggled as she leaned in and nibbled on his earlobe.

* * * * *

Everything passed in a blur as Sean carried her from the truck. He was in an awfully big hurry, something Honor was grateful for. Her body was on fire for the feel of his mouth against hers, his large hands roaming her body. Just thinking about it made her ache.

"Hurry, babe, I can't wait."

The intensity of her arousal had very little to do with the punch she'd drunk. Being bounced around against the rock wall of a chest through chilly night air was enough to sober anybody up.

Honor just knew if she didn't get her hands on Sean soon and feel his on her, she was going to go up in flames.

"Patience, Little Darlin'," he murmured against the top of her head.

Honor gave Sean's chest a mock slap. "I don't have any patience right now and neither do you so stop messing with me." She was dead serious and all the big oaf could do was laugh. Squirming in his arms, Honor said, "Would you put me down already? I can walk and it'll be faster."

"You'll stay right where you are so be still and behave."

Damn she hated it when he used that tone. The calmness of his voice didn't change the fact his words were edged with steel. Sean meant exactly what he said and there would be no changing his mind.

Honor snuggled into his hold and instead of complaining about her predicament, she did the next thing that came to mind, she once again began to sexually torture her new husband.

Honor's hand disappeared beneath Sean's shirt where her fingers played with his flat male nipples until they perked up and became hard little nubs. Her tongue on Sean's neck was just as effective although she had to do quite a bit of squirming to get there and then once she was, with her arms wrapped tightly around his thickly corded neck, she held on for dear life.

With his hands full, there wasn't much Sean could do about it other than groan, grumble and promise retribution. It was the latter Honor was looking forward to.

When they finally reached the door to their suite, Sean fumbled briefly for the keys, juggling Honor and her wedding dress until he found them. Kicking the door shut behind them, Sean lowered Honor to her feet.

His hazel eyes bore into her, raking her from head to toe as if he couldn't make up his mind where to start. Honor took a step forward needing to touch, to kiss and be kissed, but never got the chance. Before she could think much less speak, Sean had turned her from him guiding her through the room until they reached the couch where she quickly found herself sprawled over the arm.

The weight of Sean's hand effortlessly held her in position while his other hand grasped the skirt of her dress lifting until it was draped across her back. There was so much fabric Honor couldn't see Sean when she chanced a glance over her shoulder.

She might not be able to see him but she could sense him in every other way possible. His heat was evident all around her. His scent still fresh in her memory as was his taste on her tongue. Chill bumps formed along her legs as she was bared to his gaze.

Her panties didn't last long. Within seconds, they were torn from her body, leaving her open and at Sean's mercy.

"Spread your legs."

The command rang throughout the room. The huskiness of Sean's deep voice made her even wetter. Honor could feel the moisture on her thighs as she spread her legs. When Sean removed his hand from her back Honor made no attempt to move. "Oh, Sean, hurry. Please."

The sound of his zipper being lowered was like music to her ears. The whisper of fabric as it fluttered to the thickly carpeted floor made her pulse race. But it was the single-minded thrust of Sean's pelvis that made her explode.

One minute she'd been empty, aching and the next she was so completely filled her inner muscles had to struggle to catch up.

"So hot…so tight," Sean's voice rumbled from behind her.

He felt large and hot as his length moved in and out of her. His hands on her hips held tight, pinning her in the position of his choice. It wasn't long before he picked up the pace, slamming against her with every powerful thrust. Making her body quiver for more with every wicked retreat.

"Shit. Oh, shit, Sean. Please..." she begged not at all sure what she was begging for.

Her breathy plea must have reached his ears because no sooner had they left her mouth than Sean became a wild man.

Honor met him thrust for deep thrust, pushing back against him, taking him in as far as her body would allow. She was riding the edge yet not able to go over. Tears of frustration blurred her vision. She needed something, something more.

Unaware she'd said the words aloud, Honor's body trembled at the newest sensations Sean thrust upon her sweat-dampened body.

"I'm going to give you more, Little Darlin', so much more."

He could have promised her the moon on a silver platter and at that very moment she would have believed him. However, it wasn't Sean's words that Honor's concentration was focused on. It was the thick finger teasing her back entrance that had the breath spilling from her lungs.

The combination of pleasure and pain as Sean pressed forth sent Honor's senses reeling. There was no chance for second thoughts. No worries or inhibitions. There was nothing but overwhelming feeling and sensation as she was grabbed by an orgasm so strong she couldn't help but cry out.

Sean's own shout of completion filled the air only moments later as his body stiffened against her before slumping across her back like a warm, heavy blanket.

Honor felt Sean move behind her. His flaccid shaft slipped from her body and that quick she missed him, missed the feeling of being filled by him.

She tried to straighten herself but the weakness in her thighs gave her pause. It took a few deep breaths and a bit more conviction before she received her body's cooperation. Sean seemed to have fared better, although the top of his bald head glistened with sweat and his cheeks were flushed.

Sean still watched her as if he was afraid to take his eyes off her. His intent perusal made her shiver. He had a look about him. One that said the night was far from being over.

Reaching an arm around her, he pulled her close then started for the bedroom. It was a huge room with the biggest sleigh bed she'd ever seen. Sean left her at the foot then strode to the entertainment center where he pressed a few buttons. Soft country music filtered through the speakers.

The lights were dimmed and before Honor knew it, Sean was back at her side. His deft fingers worked her gown like a pro. Before Honor could give thought to helping, she stood before her new husband in nothing more than a pair of strappy heels and a silky white bra.

He was once again magnificently aroused. Honor's mouth watered at the remembrance of his taste and yearned for the experience once again before they went any further. With skilled fingers, Honor removed each button from its mooring, baring his deliciously wide chest inch by glorious inch. She pushed it over the broad expanse of his shoulders and watched as it fluttered to the floor before going to work on removing the rest of his clothes.

If Sean's white-knuckled fists were any indication, she was doing a hell of a job teasing him. On her knees on the lushly carpeted floor, Honor removed Sean's clothes then took his rigid length into her mouth.

His musky scent was enough to have Honor teetering on the edge once again. Honor walked her fingers up Sean's thighs then to his hips where she reached around to tease and caress the rock-hard muscles of his backside.

The feel of his large hands buried in her hair, guiding her head so that he was impossibly deeper in her mouth added fuel to Honor's already burning desire.

She stroked the crease of his ass, smiling when he stiffened against her. It was something she'd always wanted to do and Honor had a feeling this may very well be the only chance she'd get.

Ignoring the change in Sean's stance, Honor used one hand to stroke and fondle him from below while flicking her tongue against the sensitive head of his shaft. At the same time, she delved deeper with a finger of her other hand until she reached her goal.

Sean's hands tightened in her hair. The small bite of pain added to her pleasure causing tiny spasms to rock her inner muscles. The deep moan of both satisfaction and need couldn't be helped as she continued to lick and love Sean's turgid cock.

When Sean didn't loosen his grasp on her hair, Honor pulled back, releasing his cock. She followed the line of his body with her gaze until she reached his flushed face.

"Let me, Sean. Please."

He spoke no words in return. Instead, his eyes closed as a deep breath expanded his chest. When he relaxed his fists in her hair and widened his stance, Honor knew he was trusting her beyond the point he'd ever trusted another woman and she loved him all the more for it.

Honor rose to her feet and made her way to the bedside table where she'd spied a bottle of the lube they preferred. When she had what she needed, she made her way back to Sean where she sank to her knees in front of him.

Honor once again took him into her mouth. She tongued every inch of his length while enjoying every husky moan to escape his lips. She continued to caress him with her tongue and lips as she worked a lube-slicked finger toward her goal.

His muscles quivered beneath her hand. When she reached the virgin-tight entrance of his anus, she applied slight pressure causing his cock to twitch in her mouth. The base of his cock, held tightly within her hand, swelled impossibly larger.

Honor kept up the pressure until her finger was clasped tightly within the ultra-hot, ultra-tight channel of his body.

"Oh, fuck!" His ragged words were like music to Honor's ears as Sean once again fisted the length of her hair in his hands.

She moaned around his shaft, licking and sucking as she worked her finger deeper before pulling back only to delve deep once again. It was such a big turn-on to feel Sean's muscles as they twitched and quivered at her every touch. To know that he would give himself in such a way was more than Honor had ever imagined.

"You're killing me." Sean's moan of pleasure as Honor found the perfect spot within the tight clasp of his body was music to her ears.

His shout of release came out of the blue as did the sticky-sweet taste of his essence as it filled her mouth. His hands held her close even as his hips bucked against her, fucking her face until he was spent.

It took Honor a few minutes to slow her rapidly beating heart. Rising to her feet, she stood before her new husband.

"Thank you," she whispered against his lips just before he pulled her close and took her lips in a kiss so hot, so deep Honor thought she'd surely melt into him. Several minutes later, Sean ended the kiss then set Honor away from him.

He knelt down before her and removed her shoes, one by one, running his hands up and down the skin of her inner thighs. When his fingers grazed her sensitive clit, Honor sucked in a breath.

"Paybacks," was the only word Sean murmured before he replaced his finger with his tongue.

The initial feel of his mouth on her almost sent Honor to her knees. "Oh, no you don't. Stand up there and take it," Sean said, giving her a look that promised erotic punishment if she didn't. "Just like I took it on the trip over—like I did just now," he added before once again torturing her with his tongue.

Honor saw stars dance behind her eyelids. Her pulse leapt as the blood rushed through her veins. "I can't." Her voice trembled as she forced the words from her suddenly dry lips.

Sean growled when she tried to push him away. He held on tight to her clit with his suctioning lips when she tried to pull him up. The pleasure was so intense it bordered on pain.

"I need you in me. Anything, Sean. Oh, God…"

The sexually erotic torture stopped. "Anything?" Sean asked standing right in front of her, his eyes trained on hers as he held her face in his hands.

Honor nodded knowing exactly what it was Sean was asking. He had a certain look in his eyes. Even the way he carried himself proved just how tightly coiled he was. "Anything," she confirmed before kissing his mouth.

Sean deepened the kiss then led her to the bed. When they were settled upon the overly large mattress, he took her in his arms and resumed kissing her passionately as if he'd die without her lips against his.

Honor loved the feel of his tongue stroking hers. Loved his taste, his scent. But most of all, she loved when he entered her slowly as he was doing at that very moment. When he slowly stroked her from within, she could feel every ridge, every vein.

Sean kept a slow, leisurely pace driving Honor to the brink, yet never allowing her to fall over. "Make me come, Sean. I need to come," she cried, her insides struggling for release.

Without words, Sean pulled his still-rigid length from her wet center and flipped Honor onto her stomach. Two pillows were thrust beneath her, elevating her hips to the perfect height.

"Your ass is perfect, baby. Absolutely perfect."

The rumbled words were low, laced with concentration and need. Honor buried her face into the mattress and moaned in ecstasy as Sean prepared her tight anal opening with generous amounts of the same lubricant she'd used on him.

The feel of his fingers stretching her, preparing her, made Honor frantic with need. Her breathing came in shallow little gasps of pleasure and pain when Sean wedged a hand between her and the pillows elevating her hips so he could pluck and roll her clit.

When he finally placed his cock against her puckered opening, Honor arched her back. Willing her body to relax, she accepted as inch by inch the length of Sean's cock invaded her body.

"Fuck." The word came out on a deep sigh as Honor felt Sean's thighs come against hers.

He remained still for a moment before retreating just as slowly as he'd entered her. Air hissed from between Honor's pursed lips at the overwhelming sensation those first few thrusts caused.

"Damn, baby! I can't wait."

The words seemed to be forced from Sean as he retreated almost completely, letting Honor feel the girth of his cock head as it remained nestled just inside her body. He then made one final lunge, burying himself completely in her fist-tight sheath as he teased her clit until she thought she would explode from the pleasure.

Sean's shaft seemed to grow in size just before he came, filling her with his essence, his warmth. Everything combined was more than enough to send Honor spiraling toward an earth-shattering climax. Her body shuddered as her scream of release filled the room.

Honor's body was deliciously sore and sated. Sean must have figured as much because he filled the large sunken tub with steaming hot water then carried her to the bathroom where they sank beneath the bubble-laced water together.

With her back to Sean's chest, Honor couldn't see his face but the way he held her, the way he pampered her told a story all its own.

"I love you, Sean O'Malley," Honor said, tilting her head so she could see the man who was now her husband.

"And I love you, Honor O'Malley. More than you can even imagine."

Chapter Four

ဢ

Hayden carried a cast-laden Austin into the bedroom of their honeymoon suite where he gently settled her on the edge of the bed. The way her compact yet curvy body molded to his made him loathe to let her go.

Her beautiful blue eyes were still narrowed in irritation. "I can't believe you drug me kicking and screaming out of my own wedding reception for a piece of ass," she huffed.

Hayden knew his little Texas tornado was trying to goad him into an argument. It was in her nature to be difficult, something he wasn't sure he would ever get used to, being the old-fashioned cowboy he was.

Austin's willfulness and penchant for trouble would give Hayden many a reason to keep her ass blushing over the years, something she would fight and howl her way through. Hayden was as sure of that as he was the sun would rise in the morning. And yet, a nice stinging spanking was something he knew would always end in a heated bout of steamy sex. Life with his Hellion was definitely going to be interesting. The thought made Hayden smile.

"What in the hell are you smiling about?"

Hayden groaned as Austin got to her feet. She wobbled, her gait uneven due to the cast still covering her leg, the result of an injury thanks to the tornado that had almost taken her life. Remembering that day still made Hayden's palms sweat and his heart almost still in his chest. It was going to be a hard memory to bear. He would always be a bit overprotective as a result of the twister. Taking care of what was his came with the territory.

In a few steps she was standing right in front of him. Her large breasts all but spilled over the corseted top of her wedding gown.

Damn, I could eat her up.

Hayden couldn't seem to get the wicked thoughts out of his head. From the moment he'd seen her all dressed up, he could think of nothing besides how much he loved her and how happy he'd be when the whole damned thing was over and done with so he could make her pay for the days she'd kept them apart before the wedding. Just the thought of bringing her to the edge over and over again without letting her fall, until she begged and whimpered, made his pulse quicken and his cock lengthen.

Add to that the fact she had given one hell of a show leaving the reception and the spanking she'd earned due to her impertinent behavior, and they had the makings to an erotic night to outdo all others.

"Watch your mouth, sweetheart."

Once narrowed in anger and irritation, her blue eyes were now wide, innocent looking. "What's wrong with my mouth?"

Hayden blinked a few times trying to clear his lust-muddled brain. Good Lord, the bat of an eyelash and the dimple of a cheek, and he was all but a puddle at her feet.

Leaning in, Hayden kissed first one corner of her mouth and then the other before moving to her cheek where he dipped his tongue into the taunting little dimple he found there.

"There isn't a thing wrong with this mouth," he whispered against her lips. "It's the foul words that have the tendency to tumble from it you need to work on."

With those words, Hayden lifted Austin from her feet, carrying her the few steps it took to reach the bed where he once again sat her down. When she opened her mouth, he merely said, "Doctor's orders," in a tone that brooked no argument.

"You're too bossy for your own good," Austin grouched, giving him a look that promised retribution as Hayden all but drooled over her chest. The skirt of her cream-colored gown seemed to float around her, taking up most of the surface of the overly large bed, yet the top could barely contain the generous swell of her breasts.

"When I saw you walk up the aisle in this..." he said, running a finger along the top of the corset bodice. His finger tingled when it came in contact with her warm flesh, sending a wave of heat all the way to his already rigid cock. "I thought I was going to have to deck every man in the place. But then I got to thinking, why should they be punished when you were the one to pick it out?"

Austin continued to stare at him with her wide blue eyes. Her look was anything but innocent now.

"And just who is it you think should be punished?" she asked, her eyes heavy with arousal. The pink half-moons of her areolas peeked over the top of the corset which had her waist drawn in tight before outlining the flare of her hip. She looked like a devilish pixie.

"I'll give you one guess, Hellion," Hayden growled as he sat beside Austin on the bed and began undressing her. Untying the back laces of the corset took a bit of fumbling. Once done, he lowered the rigidly boned bodice then tugged the whole dress free of her body when she obligingly lifted her hips.

The unveiling of his new wife left her clad in nothing more than a pair of panties, a white sandal and the blue walking shoe, which covered her cast. She was the most beautiful vision he'd ever seen, cast and all.

"Gorgeous."

The single word was growled low as Hayden dropped to his knees on the floor beside the bed. He wasted no time in taking one of Austin's erect nipples into his mouth where he drew deeply upon it. Loving the soft little gasps of delight coming from her, Hayden continued the sensuous torture on the other nipple.

As much as he hated to do so, he released the plump berry of her nipple, leaving it glistening and erect then levered himself away from her.

"Touch me, Hayden."

"I will, darlin', but first, let's get rid of these," Hayden coaxed as he tugged her panties over her hips and down her legs, removing her sandal and cast shoe as he went.

Once finished he helped Austin to her feet so he could pull the comforter down. She was so warm and soft, all woman from the top of her pretty blonde head to the tips of her wiggling pink toes. And Hayden had every intention of paying homage to every inch of woman in between before the night was over.

"How's your leg, sweetheart?"

Austin turned her pretty blue eyes on him, her smile wide. "It doesn't hurt if that's what you mean, but the cast sure is a pain in the ass."

Hayden held back his smile. Instead he merely lifted a brow. The woman was obviously working her way toward a red-hot bottom, something Hayden knew had the power to bring her the most mind-numbing orgasm possible.

"Let's get you settled then."

Austin made to move herself back toward the headboard but Hayden had other plans. "That's not what I meant by settled."

His words were low, full of the heat he felt inside. Without giving her much time to think, Hayden lifted her compact body in his arms then just as quickly turned her over his knee.

"Oh, God," Austin moaned. The muscles of her thighs tightened in anticipation around the hand he had placed between her legs. One skillful finger slid along her slit, she was already wet.

"For me, baby?" he questioned, already knowing the answer.

Austin craned her neck until she was looking at him, her blue eyes crystal clear and intense. "Always for you, Hayden. Only for you." Her answer was a breathless whisper. The look in her eyes proved just how on edge she was, Hayden pushed her even further. With curve of his finger, he plundered her heated core. Now slick with her creamy essence, Hayden brought the single glistening finger to his mouth where he enjoyed her taste to the fullest.

"And this is for you, baby. Part for that mouth of yours and part because I want to see you fly." With the words barely out of his mouth, Hayden landed the first stinging swat to Austin's pale ass cheek. Her gasp filled the air but she made no move to escape. Hayden once again trailed his fingers down to her pussy. Slick and hot, she was so inviting Hayden wasn't sure he was going to make it through 'til the end.

The next swat landed with the same intensity in the center of the opposite fleshy globe, but this time he didn't stop there. With swift efficiency, Hayden peppered Austin's ass until it was hot to the touch and had turned the most fabulous shade of rose.

By the time he finished warming her up, Austin was moaning in pleasure, begging for release. "Please…" Her plea ended on a gasp as Hayden filled her with his fingers.

"I'm not done yet, baby." He teased her inner muscles with his fingers, stretching her, filling her.

Austin's skin was covered with a fine sheen of perspiration and flushed with arousal. Over his lap the way she was, pink ass swaying enticingly—invitingly—Hayden couldn't wait to continue.

Stretching just a bit, he reached into the drawer of the nightstand where he'd placed several items he knew would come in handy. When Hayden found what he was looking for, he pulled his fingers from the fist-tight sheath of her pussy then moved slowly to her puckered back entrance.

Using a generous amount of lubricant from the tube he'd just fished from the drawer, Hayden slowly invaded her with the anal toy he'd bought specially for their wedding night. The narrow tip disappeared into the heated depth of her body. Austin's body tensed, a keening cry tore from her lips as the tight ring of muscle gave way to the flared center. By the time the toy was nestled completely within Austin's body, Hayden was sure he would explode without even a touch of her tiny little hands.

She was fire hot and smooth against his fingers as he introduced first one and then another into her pussy, made overly tight from the large anal toy in her ass. The tiny ripples he felt confirmed she was getting close, too close since her punishment was not yet over. Hayden once again pulled his fingers from the tight sheath of her body.

"Bastard," Austin hissed, perched on the edge of a mind-blowing orgasm her body desired more than its next breath.

"Uh-uh," Hayden chuckled as he rained her delectable ass with swats. This time each landed with more intensity, more precision than those he'd peppered her with previously.

In no time her hips were undulating beneath the palm of his hand, grinding into his thighs with need. Austin's breath was uneven, her arousal was so great.

With one hand, Hayden tugged the anal toy until its flared base stretched the ring of muscle protecting her rear entrance. With his other hand, he reached between her legs and milked her clit until she was nothing more than a trembling mass of need.

"Now, Austin. Now," Hayden growled as he thrust the anal toy back home, loving every minute of her cry of release as she shattered.

Still fluttering with tiny aftershocks, Austin's body felt limp, sated and so very, very warm. She fluttered her eyes open only to find concerned hazel ones staring back at her.

"Are you all right?"

Austin nodded not quite comprehending why Hayden was worried. "That was wonderful," she finally managed to croak out, her mouth dry.

"Good Lord, woman, you scared me to death."

Hayden stroked her hair away from her face, a look of concern still in his eyes. It wasn't until then that it dawned on her. She remembered nothing after feeling as if being engulfed in insurmountable heat, her body so tight she thought for sure she would shatter just before she did.

Instantly, her mind was alert and aware. She couldn't help the ear-to-ear grin that split her face. "No fucking way!" she exclaimed.

Austin tried to pull herself from Hayden's grip to sit up but he refused to let her go. Holding her close, Hayden's look went from worried to confused before settling on her huge smile where it swiftly turned angry.

"Austin—" Hayden warned, his voice low, before he was cut off by more of Austin's excitement.

"Holy hell, I can't believe it. I actually passed out from an orgasm. I mean, you've made me loopy before but to actually pass out. I thought that only happened in romance novels."

Austin was so excited she completely missed the utter stillness that had encompassed Hayden. It wasn't until he slowly stood her on her feet she realized just how quiet he'd become.

His hazel eyes were intent. Creased at the corners, they expressed much more than the unfathomable look he wore on his face. Austin swallowed past the lump of nervousness. The way her backside still burned, the warmth radiating not only along the sensitive nerve ending of her flesh but all the way to the center of her body to a spot that instantly heated in preparation, reminded her she was at a disadvantage when it came to her larger-than-life cowboy husband.

His snug black jeans hugged every inch of his narrow hips as well as the impressive bulge of his cock as it vied for freedom. The white dress shirt covering his chest was set off perfectly by the cowboy-cut blazer jacket and bolo tie. From the top of his head to the pointed toe of his shiny, new cowboy boots, her new husband was sin personified.

It mattered little that she'd been thrust over the edge beyond what her body could handle. She was still ready for more.

"Don't look at me like that, Hayden O'Malley." Austin decided to try and bluff her way out of the trouble that always seemed to find her. She didn't really think it would work but it was certainly worth a try. "You should be strutting around with your chest all puffed up. Hell, you made me pass out with nothing more than your fingers and the flat of your hand." She couldn't help the giggle that escaped her lips.

Hayden said not a word as he slowly walked around her. His large work-roughened hand caressed the sensitive cheek of her ass. Leaning in close, he nipped the side of her neck then whispered in her ear.

"Don't forget the toy, darlin'."

There was no way she could forget the toy. Hell, her cheeks burned just thinking about it, but when Hayden pressed against the flat base then twisted and pulled, Austin thought her knees would buckle.

A muscular arm snaked around her middle keeping her on her feet as Hayden continued to play with the anal toy still lodged deep within her body.

"I was worried about you, Hellion, and here you are excited over the prospect. So excited I can't help but think you might like to try repeating it."

Austin swallowed the mewling sound that threatened to break free as Hayden lifted her off her feet, plastering her back to his front, and took a single step to the bed. Once there, he lowered her knees to the mattress then pressed her forward until her shoulder rested against the cool cotton sheets leaving her open and exposed, at his mercy.

She yelped when Hayden swatted her still-burning backside then realizing what he had in mind, she pleaded. "Now, Hayden. I need you now."

Austin could hear his rapid breathing behind her. She could only imagine what she looked like from his angle. Her bottom pink from his spanking, her ass filled with the toy he'd placed there with his own hands. The erotic visions were too much, making her hotter, wetter. So damned ready Austin thought she would explode.

"I was going to make love to you slow tonight." Austin heard the whisper of clothes hitting the floor just before Hayden placed the bulbous head of his cock to her entrance. Austin thrust herself back, moaning as his shaft barely entered her moist sheath. Hayden swatted her ass again, harder this time.

"Be still," he growled, causing her to still instantly for fear he'd pull away.

"Good girl."

At that moment, Austin wasn't sure whether she wanted to wring his neck or do something to earn herself another swat. The only thing she knew for sure was that something needed to be done. She was so close and yet, still so very far from reaching that ultimate bliss once again.

"Instead of slow, I'm going to take you hard and fast, Austin. And you're going to love every minute of it. The only thing I want to hear come from those pretty pink lips of yours is the scream of your release unless I do something to hurt your leg."

The ominous sound of his deep, rumbling voice made her shiver. She was so wet. So ready she could smell the scent of her own arousal in the air.

"Do you understand me, sweetheart?"

Austin answered with a nod. Hayden evidently picked up the positive movement of her head because in the next instant, she was too full to breathe. Between the toy in her ass and the wicked length of Hayden's cock moving into her in one forceful lunge, Austin saw stars.

The stinging bite of burning pain made her gasp. The way it swiftly turned to pleasure made her moan in delight. The fast, relentless pace he set for them gave her no time to think. Every spare moment was filled with overwhelming sensation as every nerve ending in her sensually tortured body was brought to life.

"I'm going to come." The words were wrenched from deep within as her body began to tighten.

Austin could feel Hayden's length delve deep then retreat only to plunge into her again. The sound of their raspy breathing filled the air mingling with the slap of flesh upon flesh.

"Come for me, baby. Come now."

Hayden twisted the anal toy as the first wave hit but it was the new vibrating sensation that stole the breath from her lungs. Her anal muscles quivered even as her pussy clenched around his pounding cock, milking it for all it had to offer.

Once again, Hayden pulled at the anal toy and the vibrations grew. His pace quickened, the deep timbre of his voice rent the air as his cock swelled within her just before she felt him pulse into her. The hot liquid of his release was all that was needed to send her soaring.

Sated, Austin cooperated fully with Hayden when he insisted on washing her. He seemed pleased she'd managed to remain conscious this time, something Austin thought funny.

Completely naked, she snuggled against Hayden's chest and drifted off to sleep. When she finally awoke sometime in the night, it was to find the room filled with burning candles. They glowed beautifully in the dark bedroom of their suite.

Hayden was lying beside her, lightly circling her nipple with the pad of his finger. He had a fierce look in his eyes. When he rolled atop her, grasping her face in his hands, Austin couldn't help but sigh. With this man was exactly where she belonged.

He entered her slow and steady, staring into her eyes the whole time. "I love you, Hellion."

Austin could hardly see him through the sheen of tears clouding her vision. Hayden smiled then lowered his head to catch the single tear trickling down her cheek with his tongue. When he kissed her, she tasted her salty tear.

The kiss was slow and deep, stealing her breath and filling her soul. When he released her lips, Austin was finally able to say the words that had been vying for freedom.

Taking Hayden's face into her small hands and looking him deep in the eye, she said, "I love you, too, Hayden. I always have and I always will."

He seemed extremely satisfied with her declaration and within seconds set his hips to moving in a languid pace bound to drive her crazy long before he was done.

Chapter Five

∞

Ethel Granger watched the newly married O'Malley boys walk through the door of Coffee, Tea or ?, her coffee shop, each with a beautiful new wife on his arm. She might be on the far side of fifty but Ethel recognized people in love when she saw them.

The boys were alike in so many ways, and yet, so different. It was obvious they were brothers just by looking into their wickedly handsome hazel eyes.

Then again, their outward appearances almost screamed their differences. From the polished shine of Zane's loafers to the scuffed leather of Hayden's cowboy boots to the awe-inspiring size of Sean, one couldn't help but stop and stare at the trio.

Ethel patted her hair and smoothed her skirt before heading over to the table where the newlyweds were seated.

"Good morning." Her cheery voice filled the silence. She didn't offer to help because one of her very competent employees had already taken their order.

"Mrs. Granger," Hayden answered, tipping his hat in a gesture almost never seen in this day and age. He then removed the tan Stetson from his head never releasing the possessive hold he had on Austin's hand.

It was going to be hard to think of Austin Calhoun a.k.a. The Hellion as an O'Malley but from the love shining brightly in her blue eyes it seemed the pair had made the right decision when it came to tying the knot.

"Looking as beautiful as ever."

The twinkle in Sean O'Malley's hazel eyes as he laid the flattery on thick reminded Ethel of his father Collin. Ethel knew she was by no means a beauty but she took care of herself and enjoyed the benefits of looking a bit younger than her age.

Winking, she said, "why thank you, darlin'."

The blush streaking up Sean's cheeks and over his bald head was worth the effort it took not to laugh when the others did.

"I'd say Mrs. Granger's been around you long enough to know what a flatterer you are, Sean," Honor whispered close to his ear yet loud enough for the rest of the table to hear.

"Guess it's time to call it quits unless it's you the words are for."

Ethel gave a silent sigh when Sean took Honor's lips in a passionate kiss that sizzled.

When the rascally Sean finally let Honor up for air, she was blushing prettily and had no more sassy words to say. Ethel couldn't help but chuckle.

Ethel noticed Zane watching the byplay from the corner of his eye but it was obvious he wasn't too keen in pulling his gaze from Serena. She sat proudly at Zane's side, idly stroking the exquisite choker around her neck. Ethel couldn't help but wonder about the piece of jewelry the woman never seemed to be without. This piece appeared to be new but no less precious, evidently.

She was just about to comment on the piece when the front door opened. Ethel's pulse leapt at the sight of Collin O'Malley. Neatly dressed in a business suit, he exuded an air of superiority. His body might not be as lean and muscular as that of his sons but he was definitely no slouch.

The silver hair at his temples gave him a distinguished look, taking nothing away from his blatant masculinity.

"Oh, excuse me?" she inquired, just becoming aware of the fact Zane had been speaking to her.

"I was wondering if you'd care to join us?"

Collin was making his way across the room, his eyes fixed on her in that intense way of his. If a woman wasn't careful, his stare could make her feel like a deer trapped in the headlights of an oncoming vehicle.

"No, thank you." Flustered, Ethel made her excuses then fled to the relative security of the counter where she greeted new customers.

Over the next hour, she kept her eye on Collin and his family. Their talking and eating was interspersed with boisterous laughter. They looked and acted just like the happy family they were. One of the times she'd been in a daze while studying the merriment going on at their table, Collin had caught her attention and motioned for her to join them. There was just something about the man that made her forget her age.

Ethel couldn't seem to stay away any longer, so when he beckoned, she moved toward him without hesitation. It was so hard to act like a mature woman when all she really wanted to do was strip him out of every stitch of clothing covering his body then rub up against him. Her cheeks flamed at the thought.

As she approached the table, Collin stood.

"Take my chair."

Ethel had no time to protest before she was being seated and scooted closer to the table in a show of manners she was unaccustomed to. "Thank you."

She was afraid to meet the eyes of the others. Surely one look at her face and they would all know she had more than just sharing a friendly sip of coffee in mind when it came to their daddy. It took several seconds before Ethel had her emotions in check. She lifted her chin only to be met by four pairs of piercing hazel eyes.

Hayden, Sean and Zane watched her, their eyes questioning while the ladies looked on in barely concealed amusement. If that wasn't bad enough, Collin looked at her as if she was his next meal.

"Damned wild O'Malleys."

It wasn't until Austin who was sitting next to her, choked on her drink that Ethel realized she'd said the words aloud. Silence met her as she looked from person to person. When Hayden scooted his chair back, Ethel wished the floor would open up and swallow her whole.

"Time for us to go," the oldest O'Malley son said helping Austin from her chair.

The next few minutes were spent saying goodbye to the newlyweds and mentally kicking herself in the butt. When they were all gone, she turned to Collin.

"I am so sorry. I didn't mean to run everybody off."

"Don't worry about it, Ethel. They wouldn't have left if they weren't ready." Collin's eyes turned mischievous, twinkling wickedly. "I'm sure those wild O'Malley boys have better things to do than hang around a coffee shop, even one as nice as yours."

He pushed his seat away from the table then helped Ethel from hers. His voice was low and gravelly in her ear. "Tell that wonderful employee of yours you'll be back later."

Shivers crept up Ethel's spine when Collin's hand settled at her lower back. He led her to the counter where she had a few words with her employee.

Collin seemed pleased when she'd finished her conversation. His mouth closed in on hers, stopping just a breath away from her lips. "This wild O'Malley can think of a few things he'd rather be doing than sipping coffee, too."

As they headed out the door, Ethel's body quaked in anticipation. She couldn't think of anything better than learning firsthand all about getting O'Malley wild.

Enjoy an excerpt from:
SEX, SPIES AND SAPPHIRE

Sarah Walsh zipped her red convertible into a gap between a sedan and a black London cab and sped down Bayswater Road, heading toward Notting Hill. The wind tugged at her dark curls and the early spring sunshine made her feel pleasantly warm. She warbled a few notes of a top-ten hit then stopped to laugh with the sheer pleasure of being alive. It was a great day to be in the spy business.

Shifting down a gear, she made a left turn and five minutes later pulled up in Drayson Mews. Sarah leapt from her vehicle, grabbed her bag and strode over to the sparkling white door. She stabbed the polished brass button to the right of the door with her finger and leaned forward to speak into the intercom. "It's Sarah. I've come to see grandmother." Code to announce she had arrived for a meeting with Mr. Mark, the London head of Spies Anonymous.

She waited, a smile playing across her lips when envisaging the young male who would answer the door. Cute in a scholarly kind of way, Chester always blushed in her presence, especially if she flirted or teasingly leaned close and brushed a kiss across his freshly shaven cheek.

Footsteps sounded and the door flew open. Full of devilment, Sarah puckered up ready to give him the kiss of his life. But it wasn't Chester on the other side and her kiss landed on the lined cheek of Mr. Mark, her boss.

"Oops." Sarah made a moue of disappointment even as she secretly laughed at the red imprint her lipstick had left. Mr. Mark was no fun, but maybe not all was lost. She glanced past her boss. "Where's Chester?"

"About time. Come along, Walsh. My office. Now. We have a matter of grave national importance before us. No time for your shenanigans."

Sarah sobered rapidly, her curiosity piqued by his words. What would this particular mission bring? She followed him up the narrow carpeted stairs to the luxurious office on the first floor. One of her fellow operatives and very good friend

Thomas MacIntyre lounged in a cream leather chair. He straightened and stood when they entered the room, winking at Sarah when Mr. Mark wasn't looking. A traditionally tall and delicious man with military short dark hair, a profile that spoke of power and a jaw that hinted at determination, he was also a lot of fun, if a person made an effort to chip away at the aristocratic reserve first. Sarah grinned, a zinger of awareness spearing through her body. A great deal of fun. Thomas' dark gaze dropped to her breasts for an instant before rising again to study her mouth. To her consternation, Sarah felt her nipples tighten against the silky fabric of her new red camisole. In an effort to hide the reaction, she turned to toss her handbag until she required it again. The black leather bag flew in a graceful arc, strap landing on the coat stand seconds before Sarah took a seat beside Thomas. *Yes!*

"No time for your games, Walsh."

Thomas' dark eyes twinkled. "Sarah thinks life is one long game."

"Of course it is." Sarah gave an emphatic nod. "Where's the fun in being serious all the time?"

Mr. Mark scowled his disapproval but refrained from speaking again. Instead, he moved behind the large oak desk dominating the room and dropped into an executive leather chair. He came straight to the point, his serious mien highlighting the importance of the mission he was about to give them. "Last month, the Commonwealth Heads of State meeting was held in Sydney, Australia. Yesterday, sources informed us that senior members of the British party had compromising photos taken of them during a…ah…private moment. The people responsible are demanding we withdraw our troops from Mundavia, plus they want three billion Euros in exchange for the photos and negatives."

Mr. Mark dimmed the lights and flicked a switch to open a small screen on the wall to the side of his desk. Images of Julie Mortimer, the British prime minister, and Toby Longstreet, her senior aide, flashed up on the screen attached to the wall. Their faces were close. Julie wore an intimate smile that took her from studious and clever to sex siren while Toby Longstreet appeared plain besotted. It was very obvious they were more than coworkers.

"I interrupted my game of golf for this?" Thomas drawled, fiddling with one of his gold cufflinks. "Why don't they just suck it up and deal with the tabloid speculation?"

Sarah remained quiet even though she agreed with Thomas. She couldn't see what the problem was since both the prime minister and her aide were single and unattached.

Their boss clicked on a button of his laptop computer and the image changed. This time there were three people in the picture. In addition to Julie Mortimer and Toby Longstreet there was another man. Sarah's breath caught as she studied the second male.

"Ah, I see you recognize our third player." Mr. Mark sounded smug.

Sarah willed herself to remain impassive while inwardly she cursed the small sound that had given her away. She knew better than to give Mr. Mark an opening like that. "Flynn Wangford. We clashed during my last assignment."

Why an electronic book?

We live in the Information Age — an exciting time in the history of human civilization, in which technology rules supreme and continues to progress in leaps and bounds every minute of every day. For a multitude of reasons, more and more avid literary fans are opting to purchase e-books instead of paper books. The question from those not yet initiated into the world of electronic reading is simply: *Why?*

1. *Price.* An electronic title at Ellora's Cave Publishing and Cerridwen Press runs anywhere from 40% to 75% less than the cover price of the exact same title in paperback format. Why? Basic mathematics and cost. It is less expensive to publish an e-book (no paper and printing, no warehousing and shipping) than it is to publish a paperback, so the savings are passed along to the consumer.

2. *Space.* Running out of room in your house for your books? That is one worry you will never have with electronic books. For a low one-time cost, you can purchase a handheld device specifically designed for e-reading. Many e-readers have large, convenient screens for viewing. Better yet, hundreds of titles can be stored within your new library — on a single microchip. There are a variety of e-readers from different manufacturers. You can also read e-books on your PC or laptop computer. (Please note that Ellora's Cave does not endorse any specific brands.

You can check our websites at www.ellorascave.com or www.cerridwenpress.com for information we make available to new consumers.)

3. *Mobility*.   Because your new e-library consists of only a microchip within a small, easily transportable e-reader, your entire cache of books can be taken with you wherever you go.

4. ***Personal Viewing Preferences.***   Are the words you are currently reading too small? Too large? Too… ANNOYING? Paperback books cannot be modified according to personal preferences, but e-books can.

5. ***Instant Gratification.***   Is it the middle of the night and all the bookstores near you are closed? Are you tired of waiting days, sometimes weeks, for bookstores to ship the novels you bought? Ellora's Cave Publishing sells instantaneous downloads twenty-four hours a day, seven days a week, every day of the year. Our webstore is never closed. Our e-book delivery system is 100% automated, meaning your order is filled as soon as you pay for it.

Those are a few of the top reasons why electronic books are replacing paperbacks for many avid readers.

As always, Ellora's Cave and Cerridwen Press welcome your questions and comments. We invite you to email us at Comments@ellorascave.com or write to us directly at Ellora's Cave Publishing Inc., 1056 Home Avenue, Akron, OH 44310-3502.

Discover for yourself why readers can't get enough
of the multiple award-winning publisher
Ellora's Cave.

Whether you prefer e-books or paperbacks,

be sure to visit EC on the web at
www.ellorascave.com

for an erotic reading experience that will leave you
breathless.